The Montana Doctor

The Montana Doctor

A Grand, Montana Romance

Paula Altenburg

TULE
PUBLISHING

Dedication

For Robin Fulton. We can't thank you enough for your kindness and everything you've done.

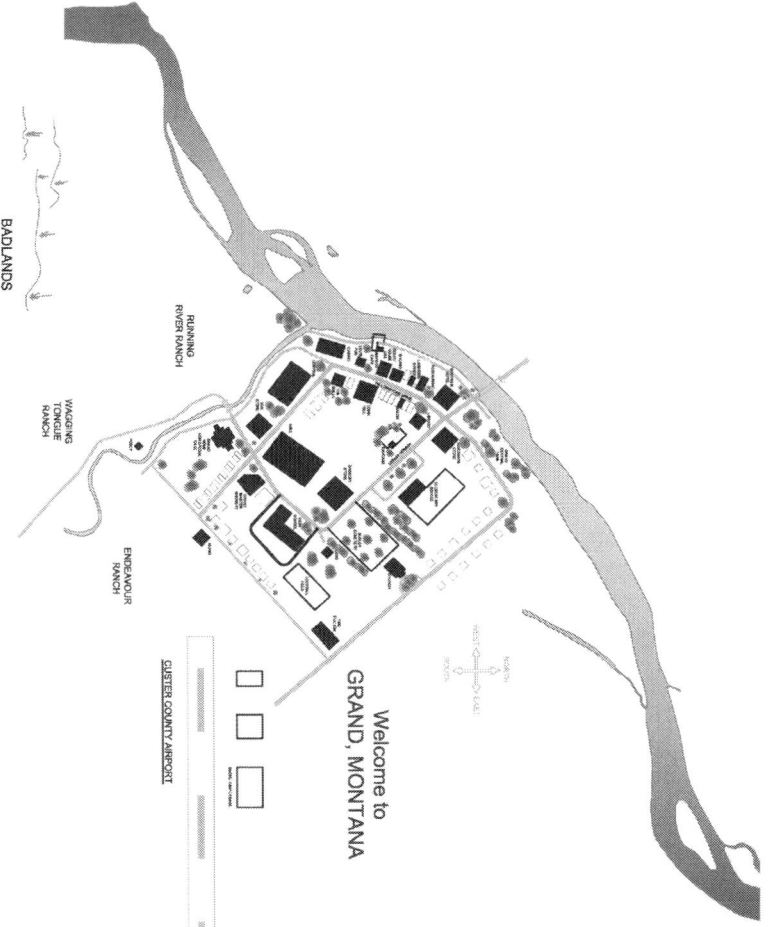

Welcome to
GRAND, MONTANA

BADLANDS

RUNNING
RIVER RANCH

WAGGING
TONGUE
RANCH

ENDEAVOUR
RANCH

NORTH

WEST—EAST

SOUTH

CUSTER COUNTY AIRPORT

Chapter One

Hannah

"I'LL KILL HIM," Blaise said.

Her brother wore a smile for the benefit of anyone watching, but Hannah Brand knew he was serious. As a teenager, he'd always been too quick with his fists. Maybe the meet-and-greet for their baby sister's bridal party hadn't been the best place to tell him about Tim's affair, but he'd asked why Tim wasn't with her and she'd stumbled.

Heat stretched the skin too tight on her cheeks as she struggled through a fresh wave of shock over discovering someone she'd loved since she was fifteen had cheated on her with a woman from his work. Then, since getting that off his chest must have felt good, he'd told her there'd been another girl right after they'd first moved in together.

She didn't tell Blaise that part, though. She didn't want him going to prison.

"Don't say anything, please," she begged him. "I don't want to upset Alayna." Not so close to the wedding, when Alayna was already stressed about her mother-in-law-to-be's control issues. Mrs. Campbell had turned the wedding into Sweetheart's social event of the year and poor, shy Alayna was out of her depth.

"Alayna is fine. Tim's the one you should worry about." Blaise tossed a piece of cubed cheese from the buffet beside them into his mouth. "I've always hated that asshole."

Hannah hated him too, and for more than the affairs, although those were definitely the worst. They'd been in the process of buying a building in Grand, Montana, to convert into a brewery. She'd worked hard to become the head brewer at her job in Bozeman in preparation. She'd put him through college so he could manage their business. She'd drafted the business plan he'd used as a class project. They'd been set to move out on their own. And now this.

"Where does this leave you and your brewery?" Blaise asked, tapping into her thoughts with the uncanny sixth sense of a sibling.

"I don't know," she admitted.

Blaise's gaze drilled into her. "Don't give up on your dreams, Hannah. You don't need him. You never did. He needed you." Their older brother Damon, across the main room in the Bar-No Sweetheart Ranch lodge where the Campbells were hosting the party, raised an arm and signaled for Blaise to join him and the groom. They were up to something—something to do with the wedding—but Hannah didn't know what. "Don't you give up," Blaise commanded again, touching her arm.

He moved off, leaving her alone at the buffet. She clutched her empty plate like a shield, summoned a smile she didn't feel, and prepared to mingle with other guests. The crowd was small, confined to the bridal party and their significant others.

She no longer had one of those. A flutter of panic tickled her throat. She didn't know how to be single. Maybe she could sneak out without anyone noticing. Blaise would make excuses for her.

Before she could act, one of the groomsmen approached the buffet and cut off her exit. They'd never met, but since she'd met everyone else, he had to be Dallas Tucker. Alayna talked about him quite a bit. He liked to tease her—probably because she was shy—and she thought he was funny. He'd recently opened a small medical practice in Sweetheart.

Alayna hadn't mentioned how attractive he was, however. Tall, with black, curly hair, and direct hazel eyes set against sharp cheekbones and full, sexy lips, he looked more like an underwear model than a small-town family physician.

And he was looking at her in a way that said he liked what he saw.

"Hey," he said, leaning past her to grab a plate. His shoulder brushed hers—cool, crisp cotton against bare, sensitive skin. "You must be Hannah. I hear you and I will be walking down the aisle together."

Funny. She saw why Alayna liked him so much.

"And you must be Dallas. Alayna calls you Doctor Dancy Pants," she replied, blurting it out because her brain couldn't believe he was flirting with her and didn't know how to react.

"Not to his face, I don't!" Alayna, who was standing within earshot, protested, her cheeks turning bright red.

"Interesting," Dallas said, still focused on Hannah. Amusement, not embarrassment, colored his tone. "Did she explain why?"

"No, but I assumed it's because you like to dance."

"I do. In fact..." He dug out his phone, flicked his thumb over the screen, and seconds later, her favorite James Arthur song had heads turning toward them. He tucked the phone into his shirt pocket. Then he took her empty plate and set it on the table along with the one he hadn't used. "If we're going to hit the floor at the wedding together, I think we should put in some practice while we still can. What do you say?"

Her stupid brain came up blank. She'd run out of witty responses. Spontaneity wasn't one of her strengths and she'd used up about thirty years' worth of reserves. And while it was flattering, particularly right now, Dr. Tucker was coming on a bit stronger than she was used to, as well.

Then, she heard Tim's voice in her head. *"All you do is work. You aren't any fun, anymore. When's the last time we had sex?"*

They might have had it more often if he wasn't already having it with somebody else.

Something inside Hannah snapped. She could be fun. She could be spontaneous and bold. And here was a smart, sexy man offering up the perfect opportunity to prove it. *In your face, Tim Ryder. I'll show you fun.*

She ratcheted up her smile and met those intense, hazel eyes. She let interest slide into hers. She reached for his hand. She liked the feel of his fingers and the firm way they closed around hers.

"I say lead on, Dr. Tucker. Practice makes perfect."

✳

Dallas

Ten months later

DALLAS TUCKER HAD paid for medical school by stripping at bachelorette parties and he'd had more dollar bills dipped in his G-string than duck bills in water.

But when faced with a ruthless female tabloid reporter determined to interview the three new owners of the Endeavour Ranch about the billions of dollars they'd inherited from some judge they'd barely known, he'd decided this might be a good chance for Sheriff Dan McKillop to take center stage. The Endeavour's open house had been his bright idea, after all. Dallas had better places to be.

And as far as places to be on the ranch went, the garage wasn't half bad. It was air-conditioned. Sunlight pooled in through the skylights in the high ceiling and the vibe was more automobile dealership than workshop. Ryan O'Connell liked fancy cars—although he no longer stole them, he bought them—and they offered a comfortable place to sit and reflect. Normally there were six vehicles, but Ryan, who disliked publicity as much as he liked cars, had disappeared for the day in his favorite—an older-model, steel-blue Mercedes AMG that he'd already owned before they inherited the money.

The garage door opened.

Dang, Dallas had forgotten to lock it. Ryan had specifically asked that the garage not be part of the open house tour.

"Dallas? You in here?"

"Simone. Hey." Relieved, he scrambled out of a black AMG with a grill on the front that put him in mind of Bane, one of DC's Batman villains. "Can you lock the door?"

Simone Parker was a former girlfriend of Dan's and they all sometimes hung out at Lou's Pub together. She was pretty, in a chain-smoker, biker chick kind of way, and right now, he was happy to see her. He didn't deal well with boredom and she played a mean game of darts. There was a board set up on one wall.

"I thought I might find you in here," she said. The door closed with a *click*. The bolt shot across, which was good, because now Dallas didn't have to worry about anyone else walking in. "I heard you have a Spider and I hoped you might show it to me."

She meant Ryan's Ferrari 488 Spider, custom-painted in British racing-car green, and hot off the lot. Dallas's car, on the other hand, was a four-wheel drive Jeep Cherokee because medical emergencies never seemed to happen when the weather was fine.

"The cars are Ryan's hobby, not mine, but feel free to look. Just don't touch," he warned her. "He's got a thing about fingerprints on the paint. Ask me how I know."

She laughed as she walked slowly around the two-seater convertible, appreciation in her eyes as she admired its lean, powerful lines. While not a car guy, he completely got the attraction. Ryan might not be crazy about people handling the paint, but he had no problems whatsoever with letting Dallas take them out for a spin, and the Ferrari really was sweet.

He was so absorbed in policing the paint that he failed to notice when her appreciation transferred to him. It wasn't until his lungs filled with hairspray that he discovered she'd crossed personal boundaries and invaded his airspace.

"The real question," she said softly, "is how do you feel about fingerprints all over you?"

The next thing he knew, she had her tongue in his mouth—he was a doctor, so he had all kinds of issues with that—and was tugging his shirt from his shorts.

"Whoa. Hey, hang on a sec," he said, wrestling his lips free. He caught her hands by the wrists and eased them from under his shirt. She used to sleep with a guy who was like a brother to him, he longed to point out. And that was only one of the reasons this was so not going to happen. "Why don't we play darts?"

She shrugged. "If that's what we're going to call it."

"I mean that kind of darts." He pointed at the board on the wall. It was electronic, with soft-tipped plastic darts to protect Ryan's cars from drunks and people who just had bad aim.

She planted her hands on her hips. Her eyes narrowed. "Seriously, Dallas? That's the game you'd rather play?"

Right now, he'd rather play dumb. He cut her the smile that got him homemade cookies from elderly patients and reached in his pocket for a quarter to flip.

"Heads, you have to keep score," he said, and tossed the coin into the air.

✳

Hannah

WHILE HANNAH'S FLEDGLING microbrewery rarely distributed beyond a few local restaurants, and she relied mostly on the taproom for income, the open house at the Endeavour Ranch had been a business opportunity too good to pass up. All of the locals, as well as at least ninety percent of Custer County, would be here at some point throughout the day, hopefully sampling her products.

And all she had to do was get in, unload, and get out while avoiding Dallas Tucker completely.

What were the odds they'd both end up in Grand?

Ryan O'Connell had placed the beer order. She'd promised him delivery around one o'clock—the brewery didn't run itself, and on the weekends, she was its labor—and received instructions to deliver the kegs to the outdoor kitchen at the back of the house. Someone would be around to show her where to place them.

She'd arrived right on schedule, and as per instructions, followed the driveway between the ranch house—or more precisely, the mansion—and an enormous garage. At that point, the paved drive converted to a dirt lane that led to a machine shop and several outbuildings, then curved downward to the bottom of the lawn.

She backed the truck into the space in front of the machine shed doors to turn it around so she could back down the lane. She'd bought the extended cab truck secondhand and it had a few quirks. One of those quirks was that the tailgate didn't always stay latched. She hit a bump and it dropped.

"Poopy-sticks," she muttered under her breath, then shifted the truck into park and got out to close it.

"All this time, you've been jerking me around?"

Hannah looked up. The voice was high and so angry it carried. The accusation wasn't leveled at her, though. The garage door was open and a woman stood in it with her back to Hannah, shouting at someone inside.

Hannah recognized her. It was Simone, a casual friend who hung out in the taproom at the brewery far more than she should. Hannah drove her home on a regular basis—often enough that she might have to start charging for what had initially been intended as an emergency courtesy shuttle service. Right now, Simone was getting the "*It's not you, it's me*" speech from someone much more soft-spoken.

Hannah winced in sympathy. She'd suffered through the humiliation of that particular speech. The last thing she wanted was to be caught witnessing Simone's. She slammed the tailgate again—it couldn't be helped—and dove for the driver's door of the truck.

The truck door, unlike the tailgate, had a tendency to stick. She tugged at the handle, but it was no use. She'd have to climb in through the passenger side. She practically hurdled the front of the truck in her haste, but as she rounded the hood, Simone emerged from the garage and there was nowhere for her to hide. Two red flags rode high on Simone's cheeks. She reeked of outrage.

Behind Simone sauntered an Adonis sporting a mass of black curls badly in need of a trim. He crammed the tail of his rumpled med school, navy-colored T-shirt into shorts, leaving no confusion as to what had just taken place.

Their gazes collided—surprise in his, no doubt horror in hers. A broad smile of pleased recognition stretched across his too-handsome face. "Hey, Hannah. Fancy meeting you here in Grand."

"I—" Hannah said, lost for words.

"You two know each other?" Simone asked, not looking particularly pleased by the discovery.

"We're both from Sweetheart. Hannah's sister is married to a good friend of mine," Dallas replied. "We met at their wedding."

Hannah blushed. She couldn't help it. His tone said they'd done a lot more than meet—which they had.

Simone wasn't stupid. She took one look at Hannah's hot face and put two and two together. "A word of advice, *Doctor* Tucker," she said, sticking her nose in the air. "Don't even think about playing games with the women in Grand. We talk amongst ourselves." On that cryptic note, she stalked off.

A crowd had formed at the side of the house facing the garage. It looked like Dan McKillop was giving an interview. The tall, pretty girl with the short, spiky blond hair at his side must be Jazz O'Reilly, the manager who ran Custer County airport's new smoke jumping base. Everyone was talking about her. They'd have a whole lot more to talk about now. A few keen observers who'd overheard Simone's parting words politely pretended they hadn't.

"Why don't I give you a hand unloading the truck?" Dallas suggested, apparently oblivious to the negative energy swirling around them. When they'd first met, she'd admired his ability to ignore other people's opinions. Now, not so much.

Since he was the customer, however, she didn't have a whole lot of choice. "Thanks."

She backed the truck down the dirt drive. He met her at the foot of the lawn and opened the finicky tailgate. She climbed in the back of the truck and rolled the keg dolly to Dallas, who lifted it to the ground. They unloaded the first two kegs without any trouble.

She wiped the sweat from her forehead with the back of her gloved hand and tried to ignore the clammy feel of it trickling down the gully of her spine. It seeped through her white cotton shirt and puddled at the waistband of her shorts. Long, sticky tendrils of hair, freed from her braid by exertion, clung like wet spaghetti to the sides of her jaw and neck.

Jeez, but Grand, Montana, was hot in the summer.

She lowered the third of ten pony kegs from the tailgate of her pickup into Dallas's waiting hands. He loaded it onto the keg dolly and she watched him wheel the dolly across the carefully coiffed lawn. Ninety pounds didn't sound like a whole lot until multiplied by ten.

Two hundred and seventy pounds down, six hundred and thirty to go. Would this day never end?

She wrestled the fourth keg to the lip of the tailgate. Dallas trotted toward her. He dragged the now-empty keg dolly behind him.

He was every bit as beautiful as she remembered. So many more memories emerged. His quiet voice, coaxing her into easing already lowered inhibitions thanks to a few fortifying drinks. His hands on her thighs. His warm breath on her skin. His tongue on her…

And he'd just been with another woman.

She lost her grip on the keg. It toppled just as Dallas bent down to adjust the wheel lock on the dolly. It bounced off his shoulder, knocking him flat, and hit the ground on its side, then rolled a few feet.

She was far less concerned about the keg than she was for Dallas, who sprawled in the dirt. A ninety-pound pony keg, dropped from a height of four feet, could pack quite a wallop. She didn't think she'd dropped it on purpose, but she couldn't be sure. She scrambled from the back of the truck, hoping she hadn't damaged or killed him. It would cause her one more regret where he was concerned. "Are you hurt?"

He was already on his feet again, however, and rubbing his shoulder where the rim of the keg had struck him.

"I'm fine," he said. He smiled at her to prove it.

Maybe she should have pushed the keg a teensy bit harder, at that.

They got the last of the kegs unloaded without any more mishaps. He loaded the empty dolly into the back of her truck and slammed the tailgate into place.

"You should stick around," he said, leaning against the

truck. "Dan's got a sheep rodeo planned for the kids. There's going to be head injuries for sure."

"I like kids," Hannah said. "I'm not nearly as excited by the prospect of head injuries."

Dallas grinned. Sunlight hit his eyes and brought out the amber. Holy cow. Not much wonder she'd had no trouble dropping her panties for him.

Simone hadn't had any, either.

"Believe me, I'm not excited," he said. "I already told Dan it was a bad idea, but it seems his nieces and nephews are invested. You could keep me company while the disaster unfolds."

He had to be kidding. Half of Grand had just seen him leave the garage with Simone.

"I've got to get back to work," she said. Picking up where they'd left off was not going to happen. She walked around him to get to the door of her truck.

He followed. "I could give you a call."

Thankfully, the door opened. She slammed it behind her. The air conditioner didn't work so the window was down.

"Enjoy the open house," she said.

Chapter Two

Dallas

DALLAS WATCHED HANNAH'S taillights disappear down the drive. The back end of her truck bounced over every slight bump in the asphalt, indicating its suspension was pretty much shot.

A massive headache switched from one eye to the other, then settled behind both because it chose not to play favorites. First Simone decided this had to be a good time to take their nonexistent relationship to some fictitious next level—in the garage of all places, because it turned out she had an exhibitionist streak to round out her crazy—and then, Hannah had witnessed the fallout. He could have wept.

Even in denim cutoffs and a stained, worn-out white shirt, and without any makeup, she looked like an angel. Her smile, tainted with mischief, glowed from her eyes. It said not only was she sweet, she was fun. Long, honey-brown hair curled at the tips when it was loose. It felt like corn silk when he ran his fingers through it. He'd known from the moment he first set eyes on her that she was the one and he was all-in.

He'd found out too late that she was in a longstanding, if somewhat toxic, relationship. It had taken him months to get past the hurt and acknowledge he'd made a tactical error— that he'd seen something he desperately wanted, and with his usual disregard for the consequences, he'd gone for it without asking questions. He was a leaper, not a looker. He knew it. He hadn't stopped to consider things from Hannah's perspective. If he hadn't been so wired from the performance the groomsmen had just given the bride, he might have wondered why she'd been so willing to have sex with a man she barely knew.

But he hated unfinished business. He'd actually looked her up when he was in Bozeman for a conference last fall, but she hadn't been home. He wished he'd known she moved to Grand. What he wouldn't give for just five minutes to clear the air between them so he could figure out exactly where things had gone wrong. And, okay, maybe get a second chance. He'd checked her left hand and there was still no ring on her finger.

Could he be any more pathetic where she was concerned?

His cell phone jangled out "Good Lovin'" by The Rascals. He'd programmed the song because it was on the soundtrack for the movie *Grumpy Old Men* and meant the nursing home was calling. He dug his phone out of his pocket.

"Dallas," he said.

"Dr. Tucker? This is Patrice."

He grinned at the formality. The nursing home was the one place in Grand where no one cared about his money, only his competence, but the head nurse was the soul of propriety and refused to use his first name no matter how much he tormented her.

"Hey, Patrice." He didn't dare call her Patty yet, but his nerve was building. "What's up?"

"Marsh still isn't eating."

Marsh was a ninety-eight-year-old cowboy who hadn't lost his love for the ladies. He was polite in their company, yet had plenty of wild stories to tell when they weren't around, and he was one of Dallas's favorite patients. A few weeks ago, however, he'd decided he'd had enough of living and lost all interest in food. He didn't like being confined to a wheelchair, but since he'd fallen a few times and the overworked staff couldn't monitor his every move, it was for his own safety. At his age, broken bones weren't going to heal.

Dallas had been struggling with the moral issues of forcing him to eat versus his wish to end his days on his own terms when his biggest problem was boredom. Other than his sketchy balance, he was healthy in mind and body, which was more than could be said for a lot of the nursing home residents. He might have retained his will to live if he had family to visit him, but his wife passed away a few years ago and they'd never had any children.

Dallas had zero qualms about abandoning the Endeavour's open house in favor of a visit with Marsh. He'd made Dan promise the kids would wear helmets. He'd rather play doctor at the home than rich boy at the ranch any day of the week.

"I'm on my way."

Maybe he'd swing by the Grand Master Brewery on his way home.

✳

Hannah

HANNAH BACKED THE truck into the small parking lot at the rear of the building and entered the brewery through the delivery entrance, where the rich, doughy smell of spent barley lingered. Gleaming steel tanks lined two of the walls, from floor to ceiling, because she'd opted to lower her footprint by building up instead of spreading out.

She loved her brewery. She'd bought an old brick building next to a quaint little strip mall on the corner of a residential street—mostly because the lower level had once been a store, so it had a lot of open space—and there was a small apartment upstairs. It was nowhere near downtown though, and at first, she'd been disappointed not to get a spot on the riverfront, but as it turned out, this was much, much better. The community consisted of starter homes for young adults and new families, and the residents liked having a place to hang out, play board games, and enjoy a good beer that didn't cost them a fortune in either money or time. They could bring their kids too, if they had them. She'd added a play area once she'd assessed the need and seen the age range, and she sometimes opened the taproom, which faced the street, on rainy Saturday afternoons so families could come in and hang out.

Maybe next year, if she could afford the extra staff, she could add an outdoor patio for the sunny days, too. She was never going to get rich off her business model, but since she'd never had money, she didn't care. She'd lost her dad when she was small, and with five children to feed, life had been tough for her mom. The whole family had learned to make do. They'd also learned what was important and who their friends were.

Besides, she enjoyed giving back to her community. She only wished there were more hours in a day.

She swapped her sandals for a pair of rubber boots. The brewery was where most of her work happened and where she planned on spending her afternoon, running a new Sweetheart cherry sour brew from the maturation tank through the filtration system. Between the Endeavour Ranch's open house and the beautiful weather, foot traffic would be light today, so the taproom was closed until seven o'clock.

She hummed a Taylor Swift tune as she worked. Not even a run-in with Dallas could ruin the satisfaction she felt that all of this was hers. Or it would be, after only two hundred and forty more payments.

Besides, Dallas himself wasn't the problem. She slopped the contents of a bucket over the toe of one boot as she tipped the bucket over a drain. He made no secret of the fact he found her attractive, which was flattering, and he'd been right there, ready and willing to bolster her wounded pride when she'd badly needed the lift. She'd used him to get even with Tim and she hated the reminder of what wasn't exactly one of her finer moments. All she'd wanted was to experiment with sex, because wasn't that where Tim found her lacking?

That was where Hannah had made her mistake, however, because when it came to sex, whatever might be wrong with her, there was absolutely nothing lacking in Dallas. He'd never heard of the word *inhibition*. The things she'd let him do... had been a willing participant in... had *enjoyed*...

But revenge sex, no matter how good it might be, wasn't for her. She wasn't that woman. She'd woken up the next morning unable to face herself in the mirror. She'd ignored all of Dallas's attempts to contact her. And when Tim called her two days after the wedding, wanting to talk, she found she couldn't face him either, because two wrongs definitely did not make a right. It boiled down to self-respect. If self-respect equaled boring, then she was on board.

For the first time since she was fifteen, however, Hannah found herself single. She'd never dated anyone but Tim. One night of sex in a barn with a virtual stranger, after a few ill-advised drinks, didn't count—especially since she was more than happy to pretend it never happened.

Hopefully, Dallas was willing to pretend it never happened, too. She hadn't been any kinder to him than she'd been to herself—although seeing him with Simone had banished her guilt. If they could avoid each other for the rest of their lives, then that would be great.

She opened the catch and began running heated sanitizer through the line that led to the filtration system. Being single wasn't so bad. It gave her plenty of time to focus on building her brewery business, which left her too tired to be lonely at night. When she did decide to date again, she'd take it slower. She'd be more careful. She'd show more self-respect.

Maybe she'd show more respect for her partner, too.

*

BY THE END of the day, Hannah's hair and clothes smelled like barley and hops and she was in desperate need of a shower. She had just enough time to run upstairs to her apartment before the taproom opened at seven o'clock.

She ducked through a door next to the taproom entrance and climbed a flight of stairs to a small hallway. The first door in the hallway opened into her private space. The second door led to storage space.

She opened the door to her apartment and discovered

the air conditioner had quit. Again. Normally that wasn't a huge issue, because her brother, an auto mechanic with an affinity for all things that ran, had taught her a few tips and tricks to help her save money, but a quick glance at the clock on her microwave said she didn't have time to tinker with it.

Other than the decrepit air conditioner, which was by no means a dealbreaker, Hannah adored her apartment. It had arched, floor-to-ceiling windows, original clay-and-mortar brick walls, and all of the character that went with them. The kitchen and living room area formed one giant room. Warm, pine plank flooring, yellowed with age, matched a thick, butcherblock island with her pots and a wagon wheel light fixture hanging above it. She'd brought up two black-legged pub stools for seating from the taproom downstairs.

Furniture remained a bit sparse. A worn, thrift-shop sofa faced the street-side windows. She'd propped her artwork against the walls rather than hang them. The same brother who'd taught her how to fix things was also well on his way to becoming a nationally recognized metalworks artist. He'd made a life-sized cowboy, complete with chaps and a lariat, out of bicycle chains and various spare auto parts, for her. It lurked in the corner, just outside of her bedroom, and had scared the bejeebers out of her more than once when she'd gotten up in the night, but she loved it too much to move it. She had a spare room for family and friends, although so far, it hadn't been used, and a large bathroom that also contained her washer and dryer.

She peeled her clothes off and tossed them in the general direction of the bathroom as she entered her bedroom, dropping her cell phone on her four-poster bed as she passed by. She'd turned the phone off while she was working and didn't bother to turn it on now. Instead, she grabbed clean clothes from the closet—a sleeveless white cotton tunic with big purple flowers and a pair of matching purple shorts because she loved the color—and headed for the shower.

At five minutes to seven, she was downstairs in the tap-room and unlocking the door to let her first customers in.

Three people entered—two men and a woman.

Hannah had no idea who the second man was, but Gloria and Hayden were regulars. They'd recently married and were adorable together. She was too happy for them to feel more than a small spark of envy because she and Tim had talked about getting married this coming December. She'd always wanted a Christmas wedding.

But she wanted someone who loved her, and shared the same values, even more. Those were the dealbreakers. Tingling her lady bits wasn't enough.

The customers settled themselves at one of three pub tables butted against the side wall. The tables had board games engraved on them. The game pieces sat in boxes on small shelves. The men set up a game of chess while Gloria came to the bar.

"Hey, Hannah," she said. She peered at the chalkboard behind Hannah's head. Her eyes lit up with anticipation. "A cherry sour? I'll take it."

"What would the men like?"

"Hayden says he wants the lobster."

Hannah couldn't hold back her smile of pleasure. "That one's my favorite." She'd gotten the recipe from a friend who'd toured the microbreweries in Atlantic Canada last spring. It involved adding whole lobsters directly to the mash, then tossing the roasted shells back to the boil. It had taken a few tries to tweak the recipe to her satisfaction.

"And Levi—that's my brother—wants the oatmeal stout."

Another one of Hannah's favorites. It had hints of vanilla and chocolate. She was working on a stout recipe with maple syrup that she hoped would be at least as good, if not better.

Gloria paid for the beer and returned to her table. She was short and had to boost herself on one of the rungs to climb onto her stool. Hayden reached over to steady his wife. Hannah, who at five feet nine inches was the shortest member of the Brand family, never had that particular problem, herself. She was more likely to trip over the chair and land on her face.

She drew three beers off the taps, balanced the full glasses on a tray, and carried them carefully across the stone floor. She wasn't known for her waitressing skills and she'd dropped more than one tray in her career.

As she set the glasses on the pub table, Gloria introduced her to her brother.

"Hannah, this is Levi Harrington, my brother. He works on the Running River ranch."

Hannah had to think about it for a second before the name of the ranch registered. There were so many of them in the area around Grand. The Running River wasn't the largest operation by any means—the Endeavour had that honor sewn up—but it wasn't a tiny spread, either. One of the McGregor brothers from the Wagging Tongue helped run it.

"You breed rodeo bulls," she guessed, and he grinned.

"Usually, we breed the cows."

"Poor choice of words," she conceded, charmed by the grin and the quick sense of humor.

Levi was blond haired, blue eyed, and possessed a scruff of beard on his chin and cheeks that leaned toward red. Biceps bulged under the rolled-up sleeves of a red-checkered shirt and he had the deep tan and work-roughened hands of a man who spent most of his days outdoors. He was a cowboy—no doubt about that. There was something inherently loveable about them, despite the overdose of testosterone the universe had gifted them with.

Hannah loved getting to know her customers and never hesitated to stop and talk, especially when business was slow, as it was this early in the evening. But the way Gloria's eyes flitted between Levi and her made her wary. Since she'd moved to Grand, a few of the older local women had tried fixing her up with their sons and nephews and she'd learned to recognize the signs. She'd managed to avoid their efforts so far, but no one had brought a man to the taproom before.

A trickle of panic infiltrated her heart. She'd been with Tim for almost half her life and she couldn't imagine that same level of intimacy with anyone else. A vision of black, shaggy curls and warm, hazel eyes popped into her head. She pushed it away. What happened with Dallas didn't count.

"Enjoy your drinks," she said hastily, then almost ran for the safety of the bar.

Stupid.

She was so stupid. Tim hadn't let fifteen years together stop him from finding somebody else. She had to move on, too. But this wasn't the night. It had been less than a year, after all. She had plenty of time to get past the damage he'd done to her self-esteem.

More customers entered the taproom. Soon, all of the tables were full and Hannah was too busy to worry about her relationship status.

She loaded another tray and wound her way through the tables, delivering drinks.

"You have a nice place," a warm voice said from behind her as she set the empty tray on the bar.

Hannah looked up. It was Levi.

"The stout is amazing," he added, holding up his half-empty glass.

"Thank you." She lifted the bar flap and ducked through.

He leaned half-across the bar, taking his weight on his forearms. "I'm going to level with you. Gloria is pressuring me to ask you out." The spark of humor that flashed in his eyes said he realized how that must have sounded. "Don't get me wrong. I want to ask," he added quickly. "I don't want you to say yes just to save me from my sister, though. She's a bully, by the way. Has been her whole life. For as long as I can remember. But that's my problem, not yours."

Hannah couldn't suppress the twitch of her lips because she wanted so badly to laugh. "Really? She doesn't seem as if she could take you in a fair fight."

"Not since I was twelve and hit my first growth spurt," he said, sagely nodding agreement. "But she fights dirty and she's got Hayden in her corner now. I'm not as certain I can take him."

The thought of either Hayden or Gloria involved in a brawl defied even her vivid imagination and she gave in to her laugh. It rolled out of her belly and erupted from her throat, causing a few heads to turn.

Levi, encouraged, continued. "She wants to see me settled with babies so our kids can play together. That's getting a little ahead of things, though. I'd settle for a cup of coffee, or maybe dinner, for starters."

Hannah's laugh died. While flattered that he was asking her out, it would be unfair of her to say yes. On the surface he seemed quiet and friendly, with a great sense of humor, and yet, red flags were waving all over the place. She'd grown up in a small town filled with cowboys and there was no doubt in her mind that someone steady, like Levi, who watched his sister and her husband with a particular look on his face, wanted what they had. She understood. She wanted it too. But, as cute and funny as he was, he didn't spark the slightest bit of romantic interest in her.

Besides, it would be a long time before she ever trusted another man with her heart. Levi might as well expend his efforts on someone less... burned. She opened her mouth to say no and make her excuses. *"I just got out of a long-term relationship and it's too soon. Maybe some other time."*

But the outer door opened and her lungs shriveled like punctured balloons.

A tall figure, topped with black, shaggy curls and direct hazel eyes, scanned the crowd. His eyes zoomed in on her as if there were no one else in the room, and her knees served notice they were going on strike, because the heat directed at her made her lady bits do a lot more than tingle. She gripped the bar for support. It was the same look that had brought on her reckless behavior at her sister's wedding, when she'd thrown common sense through the window and hiked her skirt to her waist in a barn. It brought back the feel of the strong, smooth glide of his hands. The taste of his lips. The way he felt when he—

And then she recalled the morning-after sense of self-loathing that she'd never quite shaken. For weeks after learning he'd relocated to Grand, she'd wondered what she'd do if he ever dropped by. When he hadn't, she'd assumed the taproom setting didn't suit his new, billionaire style. Neither did she.

Now he was here. What did he want?

Levi half-turned to see what had hijacked her attention. He studied Dallas, who studied him back.

"Oh," Levi said slowly, as if he understood something he most definitely did not.

"I'd love to have coffee with you," she blurted out.

Chapter Three

Hannah

L EVI LOOKED AS surprised as she felt.

No wonder. That certainly wasn't what she'd intended to say, and for a stomach-churning split second, she feared he might call her on it.

"How about I swing by and pick you up around eleven tomorrow morning?" he suggested, kindly pretending not to notice the way she'd shifted gears.

Meanwhile Hannah, her tongue thick with dread, could do nothing but nod, because Dallas, with the complete lack of self-consciousness that contributed to his larger-than-life personality, had set a course for the bar, oblivious to the way the entire room had gone silent.

Maybe people weren't comfortable sharing drinks with their doctor. More likely they wondered what a billionaire was doing in the Grand Master Brewery, which wasn't a five-star establishment. There was no food on the menu and patrons receiving takeout deliveries was common.

He reached the bar, where she didn't have stools, only a

foot rail, because when things got busy, the regulars knew to pick up their own drinks and skedaddle and save her having to deliver to tables.

"Hey, Levi," Dallas said, leaning against the bar so that he faced the other man, effectively cutting Hannah out of the conversation, to her irritation.

Levi bobbed his chin. "Doc."

The friendliness of his tone suggested he liked Dallas, which wasn't surprising. Everyone liked him. Hannah had liked him too, right up until he became a glaring reminder of her attempt to be something she wasn't at an especially low point in her life. Now she just felt awkward and embarrassed around him.

Dallas gestured at Levi's now-empty glass. "What are you drinking?"

"The stout."

He formed a vee with his fingers and waved them at Hannah. "We'll take two."

Hannah's own fingers turned into thumbs. She wasn't at all comfortable with Dallas and the man she'd just agreed to go out with having a few drinks together and she sloshed the beer from the tap down the sides of the glass as she poured. She sopped up the spill with a towel and handed the beer to the men.

In return, Dallas passed her an Amex black card so she could start him a tab. She tried not to goggle. She'd heard of them, but this was the first she'd ever seen in real life. She'd half-expected it to come with its own personal security detail.

She ran the card through her point-of-sale terminal with a reverence that reminded her Dallas was out of her league, had likely forgotten all about the night of the wedding, and in fact, maybe she should be flattered he'd managed to remember her name. She wasn't, though. On the mixed emotions scale, she was leaning more toward annoyance. Why was he here?

Because if it was for her, no one would guess.

She returned his card to him and he tucked it into his wallet, then haphazardly jammed his wallet into a back pocket while she hovered, trying to figure it out.

The two men were discussing Tennessee Walkers, a breed she disliked. They walked too fast and their gait looked jerky, not pretty, although she conceded their ride was smooth enough. She didn't care for a show industry that encouraged disreputable breeders to train them with weights and acids to heighten their step either, a practice called soring, which continued to this day, no matter how illegal the practice might be.

The talk shifted from horses to bulls, then moved on to dairy prices, and just when Hannah thought the pair of them couldn't get any more boring, the topic of anaerobic digestion biomass powerplants cropped up. The Wagging Tongue Ranch had installed one and Levi was a huge fan.

Since Hannah could drone on about brewing, she understood—but it looked like she and Levi would both need that coffee tomorrow morning to get through their date, because the conversation alone would never keep them awake. She knew a bit about horses, only because what teenaged girl didn't love to ride, but next to nothing about dairy farming and cattle. Her palms started to sweat. She knew even less about dating. How had she gotten herself into this mess?

Alayna's wedding. That was how.

Finally, after over an hour of listening in, afraid the conversation might turn to how she and Dallas knew each other at any moment, Gloria approached the two men and tapped her brother on the shoulder. "I hate to interrupt," she said to him, "but it's late and we're heading home. Are you coming with us or are you sticking around?"

The crowd had begun to thin out. Levi checked the screen on his phone and did a double take. "Whoa, would you look at the time. I guess I'm coming with you." He smiled at Hannah. "I'll see you tomorrow. Pick you up at ten thirty?"

Hannah smiled back and agreed, but her heart wasn't in it, because she should have gone with her first instincts and said no. He seemed nice—incredibly so—but she wasn't ready to date. She definitely couldn't imagine doing the things with him that she'd done with Dallas.

She'd never have done them with Dallas either, if she'd known she might see him again. She chanced a quick glance at him, to see if he'd noticed that she'd made a date with Levi, but he was checking out the metalwork piece that hung from the ceiling of a cowboy on a bucking bronco. Her brother had made it for her.

She tapped her thumbnail with the tip of her finger. She had no idea why Dallas had paid so much attention to her the night of the wedding. At the time, she hadn't cared. One night of rebellion—that was all it had been.

Especially since he paid not one bit of attention to her now.

One of the taproom's regulars moved in to take Levi's now-empty spot at the bar. He greeted Dallas, and they exchanged a few words about the stellar results of his hip replacement, but Hannah knew what he was really after.

"Yes, Jack," she said before he could ask, "I'll drive you home."

He didn't live in the neighborhood, but he wasn't too far out of town, so she didn't mind. He came to Grand to visit his grandson. If he called his daughter, she'd happily drive him—but then she'd have to load the baby in the car too, and Hannah couldn't allow that.

"Thanks, you're a doll."

Jack staggered a little as he went to wait for her by the front door until after last call, which technically was two in the morning, but she rarely stayed open that late unless someone had booked a private party and he knew it. He put his feet on a stool and propped his shoulders against the wall, and settled in for a nap. That hip replacement really must have been stellar.

Meanwhile, Dallas hadn't budged. He played with his empty glass and stared at a spot on the wall above Hannah's head with a slight frown on his face, his thoughts clearly elsewhere. Since he wasn't paying attention to her, she couldn't help paying attention to him.

He was what her mother referred to as a free spirit, although in her head, Hannah used a far different term. Even before he had money, he'd given little indication—at least, on the surface—that he cared what others thought. He'd choreographed a dance number for the groomsmen at Alayna's wedding that had skirted the lines of good taste, for example. And yet everyone, including their brothers—Blaise, who could be a bit of grump, and Damon, who was really uptight—had joined in. The whole night had been fun, she forced herself to admit. Every last bit of it.

Why couldn't he have stayed away?

"Last call," she said quietly, hesitant to interrupt whatever preoccupied him because it seemed to have quite a grip. He might be a free spirit, but he was also a doctor who held people's lives in his hands. What if one of his patients had died?

How did someone like Dallas, who never seemed to take anything seriously, deal with something like that?

He shook himself free of whatever it was. Hazel eyes settled on hers and she forced herself to not look away, despite all of the tingling she suddenly had going on.

"Have you ever considered volunteering at the nursing

PAULA ALTENBURG

home?" he asked.

The question, like everything about him, threw her off-kilter because it was so unexpected.

"Not really, no." She had to ask. "Why?"

Dallas set the glass aside. "I have a patient who's ninety-eight and all alone. The last of his generation. His mind is still good but his body is letting him down. He'd benefit from having someone young and pretty come in to sit with him for a few hours every week."

Pity at the thought of a lonely old man with only his memories for company drove Hannah's initial reaction. *Isn't it sweet that Dallas cares*, was her second. Her third, more practical response, however, contained far more suspicion. "Why me?"

"Because Marsh keeps a photo of his late wife on his nightstand and you have her smile," he said.

✳

Dallas

HER ABILITIES TO keep her thoughts to herself hovered around zero and the doubt on her expressive face said she wasn't fooled by his lame explanation, even if it was true.

For Dallas, on the other hand, the thoughts he didn't care about were the ones he kept out in the open. The private ones were more carefully guarded, which was a good

36

thing tonight, because she looked so pretty and sweet in her shirt emblazoned with the bright purple flower that his brain got all tangled up in a mix of lust and desire.

What did it say about him that he found her air of sweet innocence so sexy?

Spotting Levi, who was a good enough guy, hitting on her, threw jealousy into the mix, because it didn't take a genius to figure out that Dallas was the last man out of the gate. All he'd wanted—hoped for—was a few minutes to find out what had gone wrong between them in Sweetheart. He hadn't known for certain until Levi mentioned seeing her tomorrow that her boyfriend might not be part of the problem anymore.

He had to get himself back in the race somehow, especially after the scene with Simone that afternoon, because there was no way she'd remain single for long. Not with a decent guy like Levi already a frontrunner.

And then he'd seen her with Jack, who wasn't ready for a nursing home by a long shot, but was lonely nonetheless, and a solution to two problems popped into his head. It wasn't a stretch to picture Hannah as the sweet schoolmarm in one of those old westerns Marsh liked to watch. She was exactly the type of woman to give an old cowboy his will to live back.

The smile in question made a brief appearance, then she stowed it away, as if afraid to waste it on him. Or maybe she worried he might interpret it the wrong way. There was no misinterpreting her coolness toward him, however. She treated him as if they were strangers. It frustrated him to no end because he couldn't figure out how to get past it. He was the same guy he'd been when they met and she'd liked him well enough then.

Hadn't she?

"I'm not sure what to say," she said.

"Yes, would be good. He's a great guy, Hannah. I don't want to see him die alone." He had no qualms whatsoever about using her soft heart against her, especially after the way she'd trampled all over his. Besides, this was for Marsh's benefit too, and he was what was most important.

Long lashes fluttered over pretty blue eyes as suspicion of him and his motives warred with the innate compassion she harbored for the rest of the world. "He'd be okay with a complete stranger just dropping in on him?"

Nobody was a stranger to Hannah for long. It was what had drawn him to her. She liked people and they responded to her in kind. She'd be perfect for Marsh, who appreciated pretty women, but at the same time was old-fashioned when it came to manners.

"The only way to find out is to show up. Sundays are good, so how about three o'clock tomorrow afternoon?" He didn't want her to come up with a reason why tomorrow wouldn't work—like her date with Levi, for example—so he rushed on as if she'd agreed and the matter were settled. "I'll drive Jack home for you. He only lives a few miles from the ranch so it's not as if it's out of my way."

He glanced toward Jack, looking for him to back him up by accepting the offer, only to find the other man had fallen asleep on his stool while they were talking, endangering his new hip.

"For the love of—" Dallas muttered a curse word under his breath and reluctantly edged away from the bar, afraid Jack might tumble off the stool and undo the surgeon's hard work. "Pardon me. I've got to go protect an insurance company's investment. Ask for Marsh at the nursing station," he tossed over his shoulder.

Hannah, however, trailed right along behind him.

"I don't think—" she began, still sounding doubtful, but Dallas cut her off before she could protest either his driving Jack home or her visiting Marsh. Maybe both.

"It's not a problem at all," he cheerily assured her, getting his shoulder under Jack's arm and levering him to his feet. "I'm happy to do it."

He hustled the older man outside and boosted him into the Jeep, which he'd parked a few spaces down from the Grand Master Brewery. Hannah didn't follow.

The neighborhood was quiet and dark, its streets almost empty. Clouds slithered around in the night sky, randomly obliterating stars. Jack slumped in the seat as Dallas made an illegal, three-point turn to get back onto Yellowstone Drive. Luckily, traffic was light because his mind was on Hannah more so than his driving.

Every vivid detail of their first meeting danced through his head.

Patterson's mother had hosted a meet-and-greet for the bridal party at the Bar-No Sweetheart Ranch. When Dallas walked through the Campbells' front door, he'd immediately zeroed in on the taller, more gorgeous, blue-eyed version of Jessica Alba stationed next to the buffet. Process of elimination pegged her as one of the bridesmaids, and since he knew everyone else, her identity wasn't hard to figure out, especially since she was engaged in a friendly argument with her brother Blaise.

The three Brand sisters were all lookers. Claire, the eldest, was a cool beauty with an intelligence that made most men feel too stupid to live. How a cowboy like Ben Nichols ended up with her, Dallas had yet to figure out.

The youngest sister, Alayna, was generally considered the prettiest. She had a country-girl innocence to her that brought out a man's protective instincts. He had no trouble at all seeing her with Patterson Campbell. They'd take care of each other for the rest of their lives.

But Hannah, the middle sister…

While equally pretty, at first glance, there didn't appear to be much to set her apart. As a man moved into her orbit, however, her presence became more magnetic. In kindergarten, she would have been the little girl all the other kids wanted to sit next to. As an adult, men and women alike drifted gradually toward her. She gave off the same aura of sweetness as Alayna, but without all the shyness, and the intelligence in her eyes was similar to Claire's, but with none of the coolness. Everything about her screamed *let's be friends.*

He hadn't approached her right away. Instead, he played it cool, stopping to chat with Patterson's parents, and waited for Blaise to shove off before finally sauntering over.

He made her laugh. He forgot how. He did remember her laughter as it rose from her belly and slid into her eyes, where it ignited a sparkle that lit up the room. He must have started breathing again at some point, because he didn't pass out. Thank God for the autonomic nervous system. He'd never been one to pass up an opportunity, so he dug out his phone, opened his playlist, and selected a song. Then he took her by the hand and spun her into the middle of the room. She turned out to be a good sport, and between them, they soon had everyone else up and dancing, too.

After that, they'd both been busy with their respective roles as bridesmaid and groomsman, but the few times they'd gotten together in the days leading up to the wedding, she acted as if she enjoyed his company every bit as much as he enjoyed hers. He'd been clear about his interest in her, too. She'd been somewhat less so, but still, coaxing her away from the reception so they could go somewhere private had proven easy.

Too easy, in retrospect, maybe. What had gone wrong?

"Hannah's pretty," Jack, half asleep beside him, mumbled under his breath.

"She is," Dallas agreed. The Jeep had picked up a rock in one of its treads and it clicked on the pavement.

"She don't seem to like you a whole lot."

He couldn't argue with that either, although there was more to it than simple dislike on her part. Nothing about what had happened between them made any sense. He could have sworn she wasn't a one-night-stand kind of woman—he'd banked on it, in fact—and yet, it turned out that was all she'd expected or wanted. Didn't that make him the one who'd been wronged?

Jack opened one bleary eye. "How come she don't like you? You're young, good-looking, and rich. Decent doctor, too. Your bedside manner ain't half bad. Callie"—that was Jack's daughter—"speaks highly of you." Callie worked as a part-time, certified nurse assistant at the hospital. Dallas planned to hire her away for his clinic.

"Maybe the problem's with Hannah, not me."

Jack laughed. "Seriously, Doc. What did you do?"

"Darned if I know," Dallas said.

Chapter Four

Dallas

DALLAS HADN'T YET gotten used to the sheer size of the Endeavour's main house. It boasted three wings—one for each of its owners—and a central meeting area with three large leather sofa recliners and an eighty-five inch, flat-screen TV used mostly for football and hockey matches. The meeting area fronted a huge office from which Ryan ran the ranch business. Dallas kept his office at the hospital, and Dan had one at the sheriff's department in Grand, but Ryan liked to hang close to home.

Ryan's wing of the house lay to the immediate left of the front door and that enormous central space. Dan's was on the right. Dallas's door faced the main door from the far side of the room, in a shallow alcove to the right of Ryan's office.

Right now, the house seemed entirely too small.

His family had driven up from Sweetheart for the weekend, and although they understood he was a doctor and his hours could be unpredictable, no way would they believe he had back-to-back emergencies when he was supposed to be off.

Strategically, it might work out for the best. Hannah likely expected Dallas to show up at the nursing home while she was there. When he didn't, she'd have to consider the possibility that he really was more interested in helping Marsh than in picking up where he'd left off with her, and in the short term, he actually was. He didn't want to do anything to jeopardize the pleasure the old man would get from her company.

By the time Dallas showered and dressed, Ryan had settled in next to the griddle in the outdoor kitchen and was pouring mimosas for the moms. Judging by the color, the champagne content significantly outweighed any juice. Freda McKillop, Dan's mother, already had a healthy pink glow to her cheeks and Dallas's mother, Bea, was on her second glass at least. He got the impression the moms had been talking about him because of the way they went quiet as soon as he appeared.

He dropped a kiss on Freda's cheek, then wrapped his arms around his own mother and drew her in for a bear hug, lifting her off her feet. Bea was a slight woman in her late forties with eyes the same color as his. He loved her to pieces.

"Put me down, Dallie!" she complained, trying to talk and breathe and not give in to the giggles, all with the same amount of success.

He did so, but not before she received a solid kiss on the cheek from him, too.

"Seriously, Dad? Beer for breakfast?" he said, turning to his father, whose middle-aged spread tested the integrity of the lawn chair next to Ryan's.

Ed Tucker appeared unconcerned over his wife's protests at being mauled by their eldest son, or of Dallas's opinions regarding his breakfast beverage of choice. He raised his half-empty glass to eye level and calmly pondered its thick, cocoa-brown contents. "The brochure says it has oatmeal in it. Don't worry, though—I'll get my calcium from the Irish cream in my coffee."

Ed and Bea Tucker's approach to life involved not sweating the little things. Dallas had made a surprise appearance in their lives when they were teenagers, prompting his mother to tell people they'd grown up together. His younger brothers wouldn't factor into their lifestyle for another eleven years. Then, the boys began arriving like clockwork, three years in a row. By the time the third joined the family, the senior Tuckers earned a decent double income. When Dallas received his unexpected windfall inheritance and tried to share it with them, they'd told him no thanks.

"All I ask is that you look after your money," his dad advised him. "It'll change you if you aren't careful with it. You can help your brothers pay for school—that's up to you. But we're so proud that you haven't given up your career, and they're going to learn to work for their living, too."

They'd spent the night in the bunkhouses, along with Dan's oldest nieces and nephews, and Dallas suspected they'd emerge closer to lunch. Dan wasn't up yet either, although his two older sisters had a crowd of younger kids seated at two picnic tables and appeared to be force-feeding them pancakes.

Dallas dragged an empty chair away from the firepit and set it down next to his dad. A short while later, Dan joined them. He looked pretty content. They'd talked in the garage for a bit last night, and since things had gone well with Jazz, Dallas didn't feel at all bad about abandoning him to the reporter.

He ate two platefuls of pancakes and joined his dad for a beer, then played a game of tag with Dan and his two twin sets of nieces and nephews—two four-year-old boys and two six-year-old girls—because their mother told them they weren't allowed to play videogames in the bunkhouse until the older kids were awake.

He managed not to think too hard about Hannah, her date, and whether or not she'd follow through on her visit with Marsh—right up until the moms placed him and Ryan on cleanup duty after Dan took the kids to see the horses.

"So," Ryan said. They were alone in Dallas's kitchen, stowing dishes into the dishwasher and scrubbing pans. Dallas's parents hadn't been kidding when they said they expected their sons to work, and those expectations shifted over to Ryan, who appeared to love being bossed around by Freda and Bea. "Want to talk about her?"

"Her who?" Dallas asked, playing dumb. He'd made the

mistake of telling Ryan about Hannah late one night when he'd been tired and bummed out. Luckily, he hadn't mentioned her name.

"Whoever had you creeping in after midnight last night."

He scraped a plate of half-eaten pancakes into the kitchen compost container with extra care and attention. "Oh, that. The nursing home called."

"Nice try. The home has competent nurses onsite twenty-four seven. They don't need you after hours. Besides, most of the residents have do-not-resuscitate orders in place."

"I sat with Marsh. He wanted company."

"Until one o'clock in the morning?"

Dallas switched tactics from telling evasive half-truths to a full-on, frontal offense. "I could ask you the same question. You got home around the same time I did." He knew because he'd found him sitting in his car in the garage, talking to Dan.

Ryan closed the dishwasher door on the first round of dirty plates, carefully pushing a few buttons to select the right cycle as if he knew what he was doing. "You could ask me the same question, sure. Our answers are going to be different. I took the AMG for a drive to Greybull. I checked out their museum on aerial firefighting while I was there. Imagine my disappointment when I discovered aerial firefighting refers to fighting fires, not other airplanes."

"All by yourself?"

"Do you have a problem with that? Do I need to produce an eye witness?"

Yes, Dallas had a problem with it. He worried about Ryan. Not about him skipping the Endeavour Ranch open house yesterday, particularly since Dallas had done the same thing—he didn't like that pinned-bug-under-a-magnifying-glass sensation, either. He worried because Ryan had a whole host of issues carried over from a childhood that Dallas and Dan, with their well-adjusted, chaotic, family lives, couldn't begin to understand.

Dan was convinced Ryan and his mother had entered the witness protection program when Ryan was a kid. Ryan had never said anything specific, but a chance comment on a news story about a man with suspected mob connections strongly suggested there might be a link. Dallas and Dan were concerned enough about that comment to challenge him on the origins of their sudden inheritance, but Ryan had been adamant the money came from Judge Palmeter, and they had no reason not to believe him.

"No need for an eyewitness, but you really should get a life," Dallas said.

"Why bother with a life of my own when I can live vicariously through you? So, who is she?"

Dallas accepted that Ryan wasn't going to let up. In his shoes, he wouldn't either. They'd known each other too long. Besides, what were friends for, if not to give unwanted second opinions? "Do you remember the girl I met at a friend's wedding last fall?"

"The one you moped over for months?"

"I wouldn't say I moped over her," he protested, although he had. And then some. "I think the old boyfriend is finally out of the picture."

The skillet in Ryan's hand hovered a few inches above the cupboard shelf where it normally resided. Then he carefully slid the skillet home and closed the cupboard.

"The key word in what you just said is 'think.' As in, you need to think this through. I hate to be the one to point this out, but you're the rebound guy. The excuse she gave herself to break up with her boyfriend for good—because she likely knew he'd never get past it. That means under normal conditions she'd never get past your part in it, either. You'd be the burr under her saddle. The unpleasant reminder that she took the easy way out. A few months ago, you wouldn't have stood a chance." Ryan clapped him on the back. "Except, congratulations. You're a multi-billionaire now. Money makes women a whole lot more forgiving, so by all means, look her up. I'm sure she'll be thrilled to hear from you."

"You have a very dark take on relationships," Dallas muttered.

And yet the pancakes rolling around in his stomach suggested his friend might not be too far off the mark. It would explain Hannah's mixed signals and why she was so cool toward him. It certainly fit in with his suspicion that he'd taken things too far and too fast. That he'd rushed her the night of the wedding before she was ready to move on.

That she'd used him.

But as for Ryan's claim that money made women more forgiving?

Someone should hand that memo to Hannah.

"I have a streak of realism," Ryan corrected him. "The days of women wanting you for your good looks are over, my friend. You have to learn to be more careful. Take that scene with Simone yesterday, for example. I overheard your mom and Freda talking about it. They were both pretty mad. And worried, might I add, because they know it's likely going to happen again. There are a lot of Simones in the world."

So that was why they'd gone quiet when he showed up for breakfast.

"Message received," Dallas said. He got it and then some. If Hannah hadn't wanted him before, she'd only have one reason to want him now.

Except the moms—and Ryan—were all worried about nothing, because she didn't want him now, either.

✳

Hannah

HANNAH'S DATE WITH Levi turned out to be a lot more fun than expected, mostly because he'd also figured out within the first half hour that there were no sparks between them, so the pressure was off.

They had coffee, and talked about horses and beer because they had that much in common, even though their opinions were poles apart. They agreed to disagree on sour "girlie" beer, as he called it, and whether or not Tennessee Walkers qualified as a breed.

As a result, she arrived at the Grand Manor nursing home less concerned as to what Dallas's motives might be. It was a beautiful day and the possibility of a lonely old man without any interest in enjoying it broke her heart.

The nursing home wasn't far from the hospital. Care had been taken in designing the grounds. Well-tended flower beds offered brilliant splashes of color against backdrops of shrubbery. Stone walking paths wound between them and around stately trees. The building itself was a long, low, single-story log structure that had been a private home in the days when cattle barons owned most of Montana Territory. The view of Yellowstone River would have been spectacular back then, but was now interrupted by the more modern rooftops of Grand. The past came to life in Hannah's imagination, giving her goose bumps. She'd read all of the Laura Ingalls Wilder books several times over by the time she was twelve and dreamed of traveling in a covered wagon and sleeping under the stars.

She found the nursing station directly across from the main door. A pleased smile lit up the nurse's golden-brown eyes when she stopped to ask her for directions.

"Marsh will be happy to have company, especially someone so pretty. Are you family?" the nurse asked.

"No. Dallas Tucker asked me if I'd drop in for a visit. Is that okay?" Maybe he hadn't considered that visitors, especially strangers, had restrictions. He was a doctor so he could come and go as he pleased. She should have asked.

The nurse's smile brightened. "Dr. Tucker? Wasn't that thoughtful of him. That's why the residents love him so much. He visits everyone when he comes for his scheduled appointments and takes the time to really get to know them. He and Marsh hit it off." Her round cheeks dimpled. "They both love the ladies."

Hannah wasn't quite sure how she should take that.

The expression on her face made the nurse laugh. "Marsh is a perfect gentleman," she assured her. "As is Dr. Tucker. Women love them right back."

Hannah followed the nurse's directions to Marsh's room and knocked on his door, which was partially open, and peered around it. The curtains were drawn, and at first, she thought he must be sleeping, but a strong, alert voice called from the gloomy interior for her to come in.

Marsh was a tall man, although she had to guess at his height because he was tucked into a narrow hospital bed like a sausage in a bun. A cotton blanket covered his cadaverously thin frame from the waist down. Long, narrow, blue-veined hands rested at his sides. His freckled scalp peeked through sparse patches of neatly side-combed white hair. When he rolled his head toward the door so he could see who disturbed him, bright blue eyes regarded her with a fierce, shining intelligence that seemed so out of place in such a frail body.

Immediately, she understood why Dallas found his situation concerning. She could easily visualize him sixty years younger, sitting on a horse, wearing the worn leather hat currently hanging from a hook next to his bed. Seeing him in that bed made her think of a wild animal with its leg caught in a trap. A nursing home wasn't for him.

"Hi, my name's Hannah," she said brightly, and stepped into the room. "Dallas Tucker asked me to stop in and say hi for him while I'm here." She didn't want him to think she'd made a special trip because it might hurt his pride. No one liked pity.

Life flickered in the old man's eyes. "Did he, now? Dr. Tucker's a good man."

He had a lovely rural Montana accent, very soft and slow, with the stress on the first syllable. Not many people spoke like that anymore. Now all she had to do was come up with some way to keep him talking.

"It makes me laugh when people call Dallas 'Dr. Tucker,'" she said. She dug her cell phone out of her purse. "Here. Let me show you why."

She did a quick YouTube search and found the video her sister-in-law Jess, Damon's wife, had uploaded after the wedding, showcasing the dance Dallas had choreographed for the groomsmen to perform for the bride. It now had more than a half million hits. She didn't intend to show Marsh the line dance the whole wedding party had performed, however, even though it was all over the internet, too. She'd had a few drinks and her panties had made several unscheduled appearances. She cringed with embarrassment whenever it was brought up by her brothers and sisters, which was often, and Marsh, who was from a different era, might disapprove.

But the video featuring the men—it was a real work of art.

"How about if I raise your bed so you can sit up and see better?" she suggested.

He nodded. She adjusted the bed using the touch controls at the base, then passed him the phone and showed him how to hold it so he didn't push any buttons by mistake. His hands trembled, so she placed a pillow on his lap so he could prop the phone on it.

"Here—let me open the curtains," she said.

A few seconds later, daylight dappled the room, she'd pulled up a chair to the side of the bed, and Marsh's bony shoulders were shaking with laughter.

Her favorite part of the video—and she'd watched it far more than she should—was when Dallas swung his jacket around his head and shook his pelvis Magic Mike-style, then the men all slid across the floor on their knees. Alayna told her later that he'd tried to convince the other guys to wear tearaway tuxedo shirts, but that was where their brothers Damon and Blaise, who were far more reserved, had drawn the line.

"That boy surely knows how to have a good time," Marsh wheezed.

Hannah couldn't help but agree. He'd made the wedding a lot of fun, especially for her, since she was there without her plus-one and was nursing a badly bruised self-esteem. Unfortunately, not everyone had his ability to let loose, then shake it off later. She regretted showing him her panties in private a lot more than flashing the wedding guests and hundreds of thousands of internet users.

A photo on Marsh's nightstand caught her attention, mostly because she'd been on the lookout for it.

"Is this your wife?" she asked, indicating the silver-framed photo of a young woman with her dark hair rolled up in the style of the day. A single curl on her forehead, paired with bright-colored lips spread in a wide smile and long-lashed, sparkling eyes, made her look sassy and pert and more than a match for the young, wild cowboy Marsh likely had been. "She's beautiful."

The old man's eyes softened. "Thank you. She could ride and shoot as good as any man, too," he said proudly. He touched the photo's glass frame with a finger, then looked at Hannah. "Doc Tucker was right—you do have her smile."

Silently, she thanked Dallas for asking her to visit. She loved Marsh already.

"If so, then I'm flattered," she said, sincerely. "How long were you married?"

"Seventy-three years."

She spent an hour with him, listening to him tell stories about what it was like for a young married couple starting out in Montana in the mid-1940s. His face took on renewed life as he stared into the past and the decades slipped away.

Wistful tickled Hannah's heart. This was what she wanted. What she'd expected to have. What she'd planned for. A rich, full life shared with someone who loved her, in sickness and in health, through good times and bad. Was that too much to ask?

When Marsh began to show signs of fatigue, she got up to leave. She paused at the door.

"Would it be okay if I come visit you again next Sunday?" she asked.

"I'd like that."

She was in the parking lot and behind the cracked and worn wheel of her truck before she realized that Dallas hadn't shown up—not that it mattered. She no longer had any doubts that he'd asked her to come here for Marsh's sake alone.

She just didn't know how she felt about it.

Chapter Five

Dallas

GRAND HOSPITAL'S STAFF lounge overlooked the emergency department entrance, so Dallas saw the ambulance arrive, lights flashing, with a sheriff's vehicle hot on its tail. It was nearing the end of his Friday shift and he'd been eating his lunch when the call came in that they had a gunshot wound, so he'd been watching for it.

He dropped his coffee cup in the sink and sprinted for the emergency room, getting there seconds ahead of the paramedics and stretcher. He didn't recognize the young deputy straggling behind them. The blond man lying semi-conscious on the stretcher was a different matter entirely.

Jesus, Dan.

A switch flipped in Dallas's head, turning his friend into a patient. He did a quick visual assessment. Dan's face was pale and his lips and fingernails had begun to turn a faint blue. His skin was cool, but not cold and clammy, which was good news. Hypovolemic shock—early stage.

The paramedic filled him in on Dan's status. "His deputy already had the bleeding under control when we got there."

Since the deputy was upright and his color was good, Dallas assumed the blood on his hands and staining his shirt and pantlegs belonged to Dan, meaning he was a secondary concern that the nurses could handle. Two ambulances had been called to the scene, however.

"Where's the other patient?" he asked.

"Headed straight for Billings. The sheriff shot him in the chest and he had to be airlifted."

Dallas ordered an IV for Dan, then removed the paramedic's packing so he could examine the wound. The entry and exit were clean, thanks to a solid point bullet, but it tore through the artery, and already, it was bleeding again. Dan needed a vascular surgeon, which meant a trip to Billings, because there was only so much Dallas could do.

He stabilized his friend, bundled him into the ambulance, then spoke with the deputy to make sure he was okay, and also, to find out how the hell this had happened. When Dan left for work that morning, he'd said he'd be late because he had to make a trip to Billings that afternoon. He likely hadn't intended to make it by ambulance.

The deputy was young and his hands shook, although his voice was steady. He told Dallas he'd been called to a domestic dispute, but Dan took the call for him because he'd been nervous and Dan knew the family in question. He'd waited at the end of the lane leading up to the house. Then the shooting started. He saw both men go down, called for backup and an ambulance, and drove to the scene to render assistance. The shooter's wife held pressure on her husband's wound and the deputy tended to Dan while they waited for help.

"It's my fault Dan got shot," the deputy said, sounding miserable.

"Dan is the sheriff. It was his decision to make, not yours. You kept him alive. He owes you for that."

He sent the deputy home—doctor's orders—then called Dan's parents, reassured them their son was going to live, and told them he'd meet them at the hospital in Billings. After that he called Ryan, who took the news with an unsettling calmness that Dallas knew from experience could swing multiple ways.

"Who's looking after the guy's family?" Ryan asked.

The question gave Dallas pause.

"I have no idea." He'd assumed none of the family were injured because they hadn't been brought to Grand's outpatient department for treatment, but harm wasn't necessarily physical.

Ryan knew that better than most.

"Can you make your own way to Billings?" Ryan asked. "Maybe hitch a ride with Dan's parents? I have something I have to take care of. I'll meet you there."

Dallas hit the phone's disconnect icon with his thumb, relieved. If the shooter's family needed help, Ryan would see that they got it.

✴

Hannah

HANNAH DIDN'T SEE or hear from Dallas until he walked into the taproom late Friday night, looking more in need of sleep than a drink.

Or, maybe in need of a drink in order to get to sleep. Earlier, the room had been buzzing with gossip over how Sheriff McKillop had been shot responding to a domestic dispute. Dallas had treated him in the emergency room before sending him off to Billings by ambulance, and if the way he looked now was any indication, he'd taken it hard.

"How's the sheriff?" someone asked as he skirted their table.

"He's fine," Dallas said. "He'll be handing out parking tickets again before you know it."

He homed in on the bar in a way that had Hannah's heart beating fast, but she managed to hand the beer she'd poured to the customer who ordered it without spilling a drop.

He leaned on his forearms and rubbed the top thumb of his clasped hands against the thumb trapped underneath while he waited his turn. It was an odd thing for her to take note of, but he'd held his hands that same way whenever he'd had to deal with Alayna's new mother-in-law in the days leading up to the wedding. Georgia Campbell could try anyone's patience, particularly when she intended to have her own way, and Dallas wasn't immune. It meant he was unsettled. Her nose caught the faint smell of disinfectant. His mussed, shaggy curls hinted he'd had his fingers in them. Repeatedly. Black lashes framed red-rimmed eyes. A vein throbbed at his temple and tension pinched his eyebrows a little closer together.

Her heart went out to him. Why hadn't he simply gone home to relax and unwind?

And there was no doubt he was in need of unwinding. Energy crackled around him like heat lightning ahead of a storm. It prickled her skin. She managed to fill the next orders without spilling anything, even though he watched her with the intensity of a hawk tracking a mouse.

"What can I get for you?" she asked, bumping him to the head of the line.

He turned a yawn into a grin. "Surprise me."

She thought for a moment. Last time, he'd had the stout. Maybe he'd like to try something different. "How about a blonde?"

"I'm partial to honey browns, but a blonde will do for a start."

She blinked as she processed his words. Was he flirting with her?

The three men and one woman standing in line behind

him tried to pretend they weren't listening in, but they didn't fool her. Everything the young billionaire owners of the Endeavour did was of interest to the residents of a small town like Grand. Someone transformed a laugh into a cough. Four sets of eyes stared at her, all innocence, when she glanced around to see who had the insensitive nerve.

She refocused on Dallas and gave him the benefit of the doubt. "Unfortunately, the brewery doesn't have a honey brown on tap. But wait until you've tried the Belgian before you make up your mind."

"Blondes, honey browns... Dallie likes tapping them all."

Heads swiveled toward the owner of that caustic remark.

Simone stood with one hand on her hip, the other patting her thigh. The look she shot Dallas was filled with more hurt than dislike, but at the same time, if she was looking for sympathy, her snippy tone wasn't helping her cause with the crowd.

Not at all.

"You'd be the expert," someone muttered, choosing sides.

Hannah had gotten good at defusing tense situations from years spent working in bars. Plus, she was a middle child. She'd been the family peacemaker and she prepared to put those skills to good use. The last thing she wanted was to have another scene like the one at the Endeavour play out here. The brewery was more than a business to her. This was her home.

It turned out her skills weren't needed, however, because Dallas appeared not at all bothered by Simone, if the way his smile never faltered was any indication. "I'm willing to try the blonde. It'll give me something to compare to the honey brown whenever it comes on the market," he said.

Silently, Hannah passed him his beer. There was no way to know what went on in his head. Attention deficit disorder might explain a few things.

One of the locals, a twenty-something named Allan, assessed the situation and took pity on him. "Come join us, Dr. Tucker. My buddies and I are about to start a game of Settlers of Catan and we could use a fourth player."

"Thanks. Sounds like fun." Dallas took a sip of the blonde. "It's good," he said, saluting Hannah with his glass. "Put the table on my tab."

She was too busy for the half hour after than to do more than glance his way to keep an eye on what he was up to. Settling Catan, as it turned out.

Simone approached the bar once the lineup abated.

"I apologize," she said quietly. "I should never have been rude to one of your customers. I walked in, saw Dallas and the way he was looking at you, and I was jealous."

"There's nothing to be jealous about," Hannah said carefully.

The other woman's eyes expressed her skepticism far better than words. "You've been staring at each other for the past half hour. He lit up like the Macy's parade when he saw you at the open house. He's all yours," she added. "I thought I should warn you not to take him too seriously, though. He's an overgrown child. His friend Ryan O'Connell watches over him and Dan like an old mother hen, too. No amount of money is worth that kind of aggravation."

Simone made it sound as if she'd only been interested in Dallas for his money. Hannah thought it was far more likely that she was pretending. The uncomfortable truth, however, was that Dallas and his money were inextricably connected, and any woman who tried to claim otherwise would be lying. Maybe Simone was simply more honest about it than most.

Hannah knew all about being poor and struggling to get a business off the ground. She had stacks of invoices on her dining room table that would have to be paid from the weekend's gross earnings. Consequently, she'd never considered there might be a downside to having plenty of money, before.

As she filled an order for one of the tables, she tried to put herself in Dallas's position. Maybe the laidback atmosphere was why he came to the taproom. Its customers were mostly young, married couples, with a few extended family members thrown in, so dating-wise, it was low pressure. Maybe all she represented was someone who'd known him before he had money.

It was entirely possible he'd moved beyond their one night of sex and was simply being his usual, friendly self. She might be the one placing more meaning on a spontaneous event than it deserved, unduly complicating matters. After all, she was the one who'd tried to be something she wasn't.

Dallas had only ever been…

Dallas.

✳

Dallas

STABILIZING DAN IN emergency before sending him off to the vascular surgeon by ambulance hadn't been a problem for Dallas. He'd also been okay with the drive to Billings, then sitting with Dan until the drugs wore off so Freda wouldn't panic over her son's slow breathing. He hadn't even minded the long drive home because he'd had traffic to focus on. It was all part of the job he'd signed on for.

But then Ryan had turned around to take Jazz to the hospital to see Dan, leaving Dallas home alone in that empty mausoleum of a ranch house. That was when the alternate scenarios had begun to play out in his head. If Dan's deputy hadn't been so well trained in first aid, Dan wouldn't have made it to the emergency department in Grand let alone the vascular surgeon in Billings. The truth was, one of his best friends, who was like a brother to him, had almost died.

He didn't like thinking about that, so he turned his thoughts to Hannah for a distraction.

They landed on the night of the wedding.

The Pattersons had emptied one of the ranch outbuildings for the reception, which didn't detract from the elegance of the event in the slightest. Most cattle operations were supported by alternate sources of income, and the Bar-No Sweetheart did double duty as a high-end dude ranch, meaning Georgia Patterson was used to hosting parties for wealthy clientele. The tables and chairs had been draped in pristine white cloths and garlands of flowers. Strings of tiny white lights formed intricate cobwebs of stardust between the ceiling rafters. A live band performed at one end of the enormous room. An open bar ran a booming business off to the side.

He found his tuxedo jacket, which he'd tossed into the crowd while the groomsmen performed their tribute to the bride and some thoughtful person hung on a chair, and hooked it over one shoulder by his thumb.

Hannah, breathless from dancing, had a drink in her hand. The baby's breath tucked in her hair mimicked the scattered lighting above them. The formfitting, custom-designed dress she wore had been specially cut in strategic places to allow for freedom of movement and she'd taken full advantage. Her blue eyes glowed with laughter from something someone said.

He touched her arm, then pressed his lips next to her ear so she could hear him over the music. The soft scent of her skin tickled his olfactory receptors and exploded neurons.

"I'm going outside to cool off, if you'd like to join me."

"Love to," she said.

He forged a path through the crowd, dodging the less sure-footed dancers and those who'd already had a few drinks, with Hannah close behind him. She lost her drink somewhere between the dance floor and the exit.

More lights had been strung between the trees along the gravel paths. The day had started out sunny and warm, but the night air off the nearby mountains was cold enough that they could see their breath. It was October in Montana, after all.

Dallas draped his jacket around Hannah's shoulders and tucked her hand into the crook of his arm because her high-heeled, impractical shoes were ridiculous for walking no matter how comfortable the women swore them to be.

He couldn't remember everything they talked about. Nonsense, mostly. She teased him about his stripper moves, which he was quite proud of, and he made fun of her shoes. They walked all the way to the horse barns before she finally admitted the shoes weren't as comfortable after a few hours of dancing and she might need to sit down.

She limped to a bale of hay inside the door of the first barn. He found the light switch. Then, he'd knelt on one knee and eased a shoe off her foot. He cupped her heel in his hand and massaged the arch with his thumb while she watched him, so beautiful that his fingers turned clumsy. He stroked a palm up her calf while he had her foot neatly trapped, trying to gauge her mood and level of interest, to see if it was anywhere remotely close to his.

"Tell me what you want," he said.

"I don't want to talk anymore," she'd whispered.

And that had been the end of any restraint he might have possessed where she was concerned.

Months later, she still drove him nuts. Alone at the Endeavour and unable to sleep, he made up his mind. Whatever bothered Hannah about their past history was her problem, not his. He had to see her.

He'd walked into the taproom, taken one look at her behind the bar, beaming that sweet, peace-inducing smile of hers and wearing a T-shirt with a bright yellow happy face on it, and the whole, awful day sloughed away.

Then he'd come out with that stupid remark about being partial to honey browns because his tired brain hadn't made the connection that it was also the color of Hannah's hair. Now she thought he was messing with her. To top it all off, Simone had to show up right at that exact moment, because apparently, the universe couldn't cut him an inch of slack even after the crap day he'd already been handed.

Playing a board game with Allan and his friends until midnight proved an excellent way to take his mind off Dan and keep him out of trouble with Hannah. Simone, thankfully, left about the time he'd built his third settlement and right before he cornered the wheat market, because who knew how badly he'd keep putting his foot in that particular mess.

After Allan's girlfriend arrived to drive him and his buddies home, however, he resumed his place at the bar. Five other customers remained, all hunkered around a tense game of chess at one of the tables nearest the door. The two combatants were talking good-natured trash to each other while the three spectators formed the cheerleading squad. Who they were cheering for was anyone's guess.

All of which left him and Hannah alone.

"I hear your visit with Marsh was a success," he said.

Hannah's lovely face glowed. "Marsh is wonderful. I have a virtual gaming system I thought I'd take with me on Sunday. I read somewhere that the games are good for seniors. Do you think he'd be interested?"

Her smile was genuine and warm, the first he'd seen directed at him since the wedding in Sweetheart. His heart slammed on the brakes, backed up, and paused to enjoy it. At the same time, he hated to see her become too invested in Marsh, because miracles weren't going to happen.

"We don't all age the same way, so it's hard to predict," he said carefully, because he was no geriatrician. "Marsh scores well above average on cognitive impairment tests. For him, I believe it's more a question of whether or not he can learn how to use a type of technology he has no prior experience with. It might take him longer to catch on to the game, and he'll likely get tired pretty fast, but he should have fun with it as long as he's willing to try and you're willing to be patient and help him."

A thoughtful frown leaked through her smile. "What you're trying to say is that, if he's not interested in virtual reality, I shouldn't push it, because he might not be capable of figuring it out."

"He has his pride, too. He might not want to admit he can't. Also, figuring it out might wear him out faster than you'd expect. Overall, I think the stimulation will be good for him. But the brain takes approximately twenty percent of the body's energy to run and his body isn't producing very much, anymore. He's ninety-eight, Hannah," he reminded her gently. "He's lived a good life. Our goal is to make sure his final days have a quality of life to them. But the end is coming. Don't lose sight of that."

"I won't." Her smile flared again. All of the blinding, inner light he'd first noticed about her reemerged, as if she no longer saw any reason to withhold it from him. It drifted into her eyes, the way it did when she was teasing, and memories kicked him hard in the chest. "I've had a hard time finding a game for him, though. What do you suppose his take on zombie cowboys might be?"

"You have a zombie cowboy game?" he asked, trying to reconcile that bit of news with the happy face T-shirt. There was so much about her he still didn't know.

"You mean you don't?"

Fair enough.

"As long as Marsh gets to shoot things, he'll be on

board," he said.

An awkward silence threatened to intrude. He shuffled ideas around in his head, trying to come up with a topic that would keep the conversational ball rolling. At the table in the far corner, next to the front window, the cheerleaders roared. One of the chess players had backed his opponent's king into a corner.

"I'm sorry about Dan," Hannah said.

"Me too. Luckily, he really is going to be okay."

He bounced his clasped hands. He'd love to talk to her about it, and maybe get some of these feelings off his chest, except in this instance, Dan was a patient as well as a friend. There'd also likely be an investigation, since weapons had been discharged. The less he said about it, the better.

She drew another Belgian blonde from a porcelain tap and slid it toward him across the polished oak surface of the bar. "It's on me. You've had a bad day."

"Thanks, but I have to drive."

He eyed the drink with regret. She'd been right to tell him to give the blonde a chance. He liked its crisp, light taste and the faint smell of citrus—he'd read one of the posters on the wall. But even though he'd finished the first beer more than an hour ago, and he was still too wired to sleep, physical and mental exhaustion factored in and he shouldn't get behind the wheel if he drank a second one now.

"I'll drive you home," she volunteered, the offer surprising them both.

Chapter Six

Dallas

THE TRUCK WOULDN'T start.

Hannah, obviously more interested in its inner workings than the safety of her surroundings, had her head under the hood. Dallas aimed the flashlight for her and eyeballed the tiny parking lot behind the brewery with disapproval and mounting concern.

The Grand Master Brewery sat at the wrong end of an okay neighborhood. The parking lot had been crammed as an afterthought into the leftover space between the brewery on the front, an appliance store in behind, and the backside of a squat, ugly laundromat. The tight narrow driveway between the brewery and the laundromat posed an impromptu but highly effective sobriety test for anyone considering drinking and driving. The lone pole lamp didn't work, meaning the lot was a breeding ground for drug deals and other clandestine activities that generally took place in the shadows. Nine of the ten parking spaces were empty.

The garbage bins, however, were full, and judging by the

smell, aged to a compostable state. A low-hanging, yeasty, fermented grain odor further enhanced their appeal. The patches of grass peering through the cracked asphalt were plain to be seen thanks to the brilliance of the Montana night sky. Not even this parking lot could dim such magnificence.

"Love what you've done with the backyard," he remarked, leaning against the truck's rust-speckled cab and speaking to the back of her head. "Add a barbecue, some patio furniture, a few potted plants, and you've got yourself your own private oasis." Because why not make the drug dealers and rapists feel right at home.

She muttered "poopy-sticks" under her breath, but it was directed at the engine, not him, which made him grin. She was cute when she lost her temper.

The strap of her pink thong peeked between the waist of her shorts and the hem of her T-shirt as she hoisted herself deeper into the greasy pit. Her taste in underwear had surprised him the first time he'd encountered it. She'd seemed more the type of girl Dan's mom called "wholesome." Now, it explained a few things. Her ex-boyfriend definitely hadn't been paying enough attention to her or her needs.

"Hold the light still," she said.

He adjusted the flashlight's position as per her instructions, crossed his legs, and made himself more comfortable while he watched her work, even though the truck was more in need of a mortician than a mechanic. "You could drive my car, you know. I'll have to pick it up tomorrow, anyway."

Hannah's head popped up for a second. She flicked a strand of hair off her face with the back of her wrist, leaving a streak of dirt on her cheek. "That's plan B. Right now, this is personal." She dove back under the hood.

He liked her persistence. If he was ever on life support, he'd want her in charge of the plug. She'd leave no option unexplored.

And she made teasing her fun. This was what it had been like when they first met—there'd been an easy back-and-forth between them that he'd truly enjoyed. She'd followed him onto the dance floor, then later…

He'd enjoyed that dance, as well. He could have sworn she had, too.

"You do realize the truck didn't die just to spite you, right?" he said.

"It's not dead. It's relaxing."

"It's got to be thirty years old. In dog years, that's…" Dallas double-checked the math in his head. "Two hundred and ten. Besides, you know what they say about sleeping dogs. Maybe you should let this one lie. Besides." He aimed the flashlight beam at the ground by his foot, where a black puddle seeped from under the wheel and blinked against the sudden bright light. "I think it's incontinent. That's never a good sign."

She gripped the frame, leaned away from the hood, and

looked down at the puddle. She sighed. Then she kicked the truck's driver-side tire with the toe of her white sneaker. "I give you premium unleaded and this is the thanks I get in return."

"Why don't I call a cab and leave you to grieve in private," he suggested. "I could call a priest, too. I'm sure Father Patrick would be happy to give it last rites."

Hannah wiped her hands on her shorts and straightened the hem of her T-shirt. The flash of pink vanished. "No need to call Father Patrick just yet. You're a doctor. What about the Heimlich maneuver or something?"

He weighed sympathy for her situation against her willingness to accept that not even Dr. Frankenstein could reanimate this corpse. Since it was possible she didn't have the money for a new truck, sympathy won.

"Seriously, I can call a cab."

Her jaw took on a stubborn set that suggested her nature wasn't always as agreeable as it seemed on the surface. He liked that, too. Who wanted a woman who only did what she was told?

"The taproom offers a taxi service to its paying customers. I'll call the cab," she said.

Grand had two taxi companies. Both were hit and miss after midnight. Mostly miss. He suspected she wasn't aware of that fact, not that it mattered. Her pride was at stake and he'd let her keep it—but up to a point.

"In the time it takes for a cab to get here, we could both

be home, in bed, and asleep." And didn't that statement take his thoughts places. "Besides, I got the last drink for free," he reminded her. "That means I'm not really a paying customer. How about if we move on to plan B and you drive me home in my car, then we call it even?"

"You bought drinks for Allan and his friends."

"I can hardly call them for a ride, if that's what you're suggesting. They've been drinking." Dallas dug his keys out of his pocket and passed them to her. "I'm parked on the street. You should try it. There's proper lighting and everything, meaning less chance of having your hubcaps stolen."

She tucked her lips between her teeth and jiggled his keys in her palm. "This is my home you're insulting, Dr. Tucker."

"You *sleep* here?" He looked around. "Where?"

"Above the brewery. My apartment overlooks the street."

His tired brain processed that information. Strategically, it made perfect sense. He'd imagined her leaving the brewery late every night, with someone monitoring her and her schedule, figuring out when she'd be alone and most vulnerable. The brewery itself, on the other hand, was built like a fortress. She'd be safe inside it unless the drug dealers brought assault weapons and dynamite, and he didn't give Grand's local criminal element that much credit for foresight or initiative. She'd also save money.

"You're living a college freshman's dream. Come on. Let's go find my car."

They brushed shoulders as they passed through the cramped driveway and onto the street. His Jeep was parked under a hackberry planted at the edge of an apartment building's postage stamp-sized lawn. It had rained hard earlier in the day and the air was still fresh with damp earth.

He wasn't surprised to discover that Hannah was an excellent driver—the same brother who'd taught her to maintain a vehicle would also have taught her to drive. She followed the river along Yellowstone Drive toward the outskirts of town.

Now that they were alone, with fifteen or so minutes to kill, he was at a loss as to how to begin. He hated to ruin the truce they'd established, but he had to know what had gone wrong.

And, more importantly, if it could be fixed.

"Contrary to how it might have appeared, Simone and I aren't, nor have we ever been, involved in any sort of relationship," he said, leaping in. "I'm not sure how she got the impression otherwise. She used to date Dan, which puts her out of bounds. I thought we were friends."

"'I did not have sexual relations with that woman,'" Hannah intoned.

"Funny."

She glanced at him sideways. The way she drew her chin in, closing herself off, suggested she didn't wish to discuss it. She'd seemed pretty snitty about Simone though, so he wasn't convinced she was truly indifferent.

"You don't owe me any explanations, Dallas. Who you sleep with is none of my business."

"Really? You aren't even the least little bit curious?"

"Not in the slightest."

"Good to know. But I'm curious as hell as to why you slept with me," he said, putting it out there.

The Jeep veered toward the side of the road. He grabbed the handle above the passenger side window and braced for impact, but Hannah straightened the tires without any issues.

Her shoulders tightened in a defensive reaction, suggesting he'd struck a nerve. "It doesn't matter."

"Yes, it does."

She clung to the wheel and took her time coming up with an answer. Long enough, in fact, that whatever it was, it didn't bode well.

"Fine," she said. "But please don't judge me." She drummed her thumbs on the steering wheel and stared at the white pavement markings slipping under the tires. Then she took a deep breath, and blew it out, along with her words. "I wanted to get even with my boyfriend for cheating on me."

He'd suspected he'd been used—Ryan had planted that possibility—but hearing it confirmed made it real. He'd hoped there'd been a mutual attraction. Instead, she'd been hung up on another man. At least it all made sense to him, now. He'd never quite been able to figure out how the boyfriend fit in. What kind of idiot cheated on a woman like

Hannah?

"And I was convenient," he said, because he liked torturing himself.

"You were good-looking, tons of fun, and I was flattered by your interest in me," she corrected him. "But cheating on him makes me a cheat too, and that isn't me." She backpedaled a bit. "Well. I guess it is me, isn't it? But it's not who I want to be."

He was beginning to get it. She was embarrassed by her motives more so than her actions, which amazingly, took away a lot of the sting. "It doesn't make you a cheat. It makes you human."

"I guess." She didn't sound as if she agreed.

A right turn in the road would take them over the Tongue River bridge toward the Wagging Tongue Ranch. They kept going straight, and in another few miles they'd reach the Endeavour, so he didn't have much longer to forge some sort of understanding with her. She wasn't ready to let go of the past. He could understand that.

But he'd like to be part of her future and he could be patient.

"What about your boyfriend?" he asked. "Was his affair the dealbreaker for you? Or did he call it quits for good when you told him about us?"

"He doesn't know about you. We split up before the wedding and he moved out of our apartment while I was in Sweetheart. I haven't talked to him since."

Dallas digested that. The only real cheating she'd done, then, was all in her head. It made him want her even more. Loyalty like that was something no amount of money could buy—as he was fast learning.

"You seemed like you were having the time of your life at the wedding. I had no idea there was anything wrong," he said. Maybe he should have. He couldn't recall one serious conversation between them. He'd learned very little about her and she'd asked no real questions of him.

"Alayna's my little sister and she was so happy. I didn't want to ruin her day."

He slapped an open palm to his chest. "You didn't even tell your sisters you and your boyfriend broke up? What kind of cold, unfeeling monster are you?"

Hannah's belly laugh teased the fine hairs on his skin. "Of course I told them. Just not right away."

He debated whether or not to ask the four-point-whatever billion-dollar question.

"Would you take him back? Asking for a friend," he added hastily, putting a lighter spin on it because he was afraid of scaring her off when they were still on shaky ground.

Hannah turned up the winding drive that led to the Endeavour. Other than the automatic lights along the front of the building, the main house was dark. Black windows gaped, a reminder that no one was home.

She drew up to the front door but didn't turn off the engine. "Tim and I were together all through high school.

We had our ups and downs, but I thought we'd be together forever. I had no idea he was having an affair. I didn't see it coming. I'm sorry. The person you met at the wedding… That wasn't me," she repeated, in case he hadn't gotten the message the first time she said it.

He disagreed. He thought it far more likely that she was only now beginning to figure herself out. She'd been betrayed by someone she trusted and had some grief to work through. He'd met her in the beginning, while she was still numb. At a guess, he'd say she'd progressed beyond anger and depression and was approaching the upward turn toward hope and recovery.

"Do you think you and I could start over? As friends, Hannah," he added quietly, because she hadn't answered his first question, so she wasn't there yet.

"I'd like that," she said.

The slight pause before she answered suggested she'd at least give it serious thought. Good enough for him.

"Great. I'll pick up my car in the morning. By the way, don't bother bringing your gaming system on Sunday. I'm going to buy one that's geared toward nursing homes so all of the residents can benefit from it."

He hopped out of the Jeep before she could protest how he'd insinuated himself into her visit with Marsh. He waved before turning to jog up the walk to the door.

✳

Hannah

HANNAH COULDN'T SAY for sure how she'd gone from avoiding Dallas to spending Sunday afternoon with him, but she was so glad she did.

She'd been skeptical as to whether or not they could start over, especially as friends, but she appeared to be the only one having any difficulty with it, because Dallas lived in the moment. The past was over and done with. His future, an adventure yet to be lived.

And when he was with his patients, he gave them his whole attention. Seeing him interact with the nursing home residents was fun. There didn't appear to be any deep, dark secrets where he was concerned.

Except one never knew.

"Oh, come on," Dallas said. He gave Marsh a nudge with his elbow. "My grandma could do better than that and she's legally blind."

"Is she single?" Marsh asked.

"As if I'd let her date a cowboy."

They were in the residents' lounge in front of a mammoth TV monitor. Marsh, propped in a wheelchair, wore VR goggles. Dallas held a tablet on his knees and controlled the VR experience. The two of them were involved in a balloon popping war while three other residents watched their progress on the TV.

Dallas threw up his hands. "You cheated. There's no

other way you could beat me."

Laughter wheezed out of Marsh's thin frame. "You're a poor sport, young man. And get a haircut."

"I can't." Dallas ruffled a hand through his mass of tangled curls. Hazel eyes sparkled with humor. "My hairdresser isn't speaking to me, anymore. Okay, it's Bernice's turn," he announced, looking around. "Where is she?"

That was Hannah's cue.

Bernice was a lovely, friendly woman in the later stages of Alzheimer's disease and it took a significant amount of patience on Hannah's part to convince her to keep the goggles in place.

"My toes don't fit," Bernice complained, tugging at the goggles so that they slipped too far forward on her face.

"I can adjust them for you," Hannah reassured her. She settled the goggles more to Bernice's satisfaction and then positioned her wheelchair next to Dallas.

"If you hold her hand it will help her stay more focused and keep her attention off the goggles," Dallas said to Hannah, not lifting his gaze from the tablet. "Physical contact is important for her."

Hannah held the elderly woman's hand while Dallas selected the app her family had provided for her to use. Bernice and two friends had backpacked around the world together when they were young and fresh out of college. Her daughters said that a safari in Africa had been one of her favorite memories, and as she relived it in virtual reality, she gripped

Hannah's fingers tight.

"Elephants!" she cried. On the TV monitor, a herd of the behemoths lumbered toward a watering hole. "Look at the babies!"

"Are you sure those are elephants?" Dallas teased, touching her shoulder.

"Elephants! A parade," she insisted, and Hannah teared up. Bernice had gotten her words jumbled up when trying to explain how the goggles didn't sit properly on her head, and yet, the video brought back to her that the proper word for a herd of elephants was a parade. Hannah scrabbled for her cell phone so she could capture the moment for Bernice's daughters, who lived out of state.

Marsh, meanwhile, had fallen asleep and the way he slumped in his chair looked uncomfortable. After Bernice finished her virtual experience, Hannah wheeled him back to his room. She rang for someone to come transfer him to his bed.

"You and Doctor Dallie make a cute couple," Marsh murmured, patting her hand while they waited.

Hannah's brain shied away from the idea of them as a couple. It would be like switching from peanut butter and jam, two things that went well together, to jam and cheese. What kind of combination was that?

"We're friends."

Marsh cracked open his eyes. They were clear and alert and they pierced into her. "I think I've gotten to know him pretty well. He comes here on his own time because the thing we need most is the one thing he has the least of to spare. All the money in the world wouldn't brighten our days half as much as the few hours he spends with us and he knows it. That's a pretty generous gift on his part. It means something. Bringing you here means you're someone special to him, and he's happy to share you with us, too."

That was such a sweet thing to say, no matter how wrong he might be.

"I'm here because he thinks you're someone special, not me," Hannah replied, even though she could tell it was a losing battle. Marsh's generation didn't understand how men and women could be friends.

Marsh frowned. "How come you don't want him?"

She wasn't sure how to explain. "You're very direct, aren't you?"

"I'm an old man. I don't have time left to waste. Each breath could be my last."

"Don't say things like that." She liked Marsh. She hoped he lived to be one hundred and twenty, although she didn't dare say so, for fear he might disagree.

He read her concern. "Life and I have no unfinished business, Hannah, and I made peace with death a long time ago. Now, are you gonna answer my question or not?"

"Dallas is…" Hannah tried to think of a good description for him and failed. "Too much." Too unpredictable. She never knew what he would say or do next. He made her feel so… unsettled.

Predictability, on the other hand, didn't necessarily translate to one hundred percent trustworthiness. She'd learned that the hard way.

"He does have a lot of energy," Marsh conceded.

Two nursing assistants arrived to transfer him from his chair to the bed. Hannah stayed with him until he was tucked in. He fell asleep again before they could resume their conversation, however, so she returned to the lounge.

The lounge was a pretty space, with lots of windows for light and enormous potted plants to add bold splashes of green. The walls were painted pale blue. Patio doors led to a small, fenced-in garden. A nurse was handing out medication to the residents in the room, along with a mid-afternoon snack. She had her back turned to the stainless-steel serving cart.

"I saw you take that second cookie, Rudy," Dallas said to a short, heavy-set man dressed in a plaid bathrobe and lime-green slippers. The full white beard and red nose made his resemblance to Santa Claus uncanny, although his mouth drooped on one side. "What did the dietician say to you about keeping your diabetes under control?"

Santa remained unrepentant despite the good-natured scolding. He slipped the plastic-wrapped cookie into a flannel pocket and leaned on his walker. A saucy grin lifted one of his round cheeks.

"She said you only live once."

Chapter Seven

Hannah

ONCE A MONTH, Hannah hosted a ladies' night at the taproom. It was always on a Wednesday, tickets had to be bought in advance, and attendee numbers were increasing steadily. She used it as an opportunity to test and promote a particular beer and she put a lot of thought and effort into its theme.

Tonight, she'd settled on Prohibition and they were going to play Texas Hold'em. Twenty-three women had registered. She had a small batch of stout she'd aged for a few months in a Canadian whiskey barrel made from maple wood for them to sample. The alcohol content was high so she'd serve it in snifters. She usually hired a bartender so she could participate and enjoy a few drinks, too. What better way to get to know the women of Grand than over a specialty beer?

The beer wasn't her only reason for choosing this particular theme. Her sister-in-law haunted consignment stores and she'd found a sequined Gatsby dress for Hannah that

Hannah was dying to wear. Jess had a good eye for style and it fit her as if it were tailor-made. Hannah had ordered black elbow-length finger gloves and a black satin headpiece online and bought low-heeled Mary Jane shoes to go with it. It was fun to dress up every once in a while.

At five-thirty, she was busy hanging posters protesting the Eighteenth Amendment and favoring the Women's Organization for National Prohibition Reform when someone rapped on the taproom's window. It was Dallas, with his hands cupped around his eyes and his face pressed up to the glass.

He wore dress pants and a white shirt so he must have come straight from work. The sleeves of his shirt were rolled up to his elbows and his tie hung askew as if he'd run his finger under his collar one time too many.

At first glance, he offered up an illusion of an everyday office worker. The strong bulge of tendons running the length of his forearms, combined with the tight fit of his shirt across his shoulders and the tanned skin, suggested part-time outdoor laborer, too. A country doctor likely wouldn't be anyone's first guess when they met him, but it wasn't a stretch either.

Billionaire, however?

"*Let me in*," he mouthed, and pointed toward the door.

She dropped the packet of poster putty on a table and hurried over to disengage the dead bolt. The warmth of late afternoon sunlight poured in along with him. His hazel eyes beamed. The pounding of her heart threatened the integrity of her ribs—purely because he'd startled her and not because she was happy to see him.

"Hey." He looked around, taking in the tables she'd moved and the posters she'd hung. "What's going on?"

"Ladies' night. We get together once a month to play poker," she said. "I make a few small batches of specialty brews to plan for future production and this gives me an opportunity to taste-test them."

"Sounds like fun. When is guys' night?"

Hannah lifted one brow. "Are you accusing me of sexism?"

"No, no, just curious," he said, although his eyes strongly suggested he was laughing at her. "It ties in nicely with why I'm here, though." He perched on a stool, one long leg braced on the floor and a heel hooked on a rung. "How would you feel about hosting a fundraising event for the new free clinic?"

Ideas immediately began bouncing around in her brain. She forced herself to be practical. "The taproom doesn't have a whole lot of space. I can only seat thirty people."

"Thirty is plenty. This is Grand, not New York City."

She really, really wanted to do this. She wanted it to be for the right reasons, however, not because he was trying to help her boost business, and she was a little suspicious as to why he'd choose the taproom, when there were fancier spots. "I thought the Endeavour Ranch was funding the clinic."

"It will. But it's a community clinic. The public should be allowed to pitch in and make it feel like their own." Dallas grinned at her. "It was Ryan's idea. I asked to buy emergency room equipment so I don't have to send people who can't afford it to the hospital and he told me to raise the money myself. It seems I have a 'budget' to follow." He used his fingers as air quotes as he said it. "Not that I don't plan to make a sizeable private donation too, mind you. But apparently the IRS has rules around that sort of thing."

"Imagine that," Hannah said. The only IRS rules she was even remotely familiar with involved them taking her money, not her giving it away. Nevertheless, she thought it was a great gesture on his part. "I'd be happy to help. I can't offer anything fancy, though," she felt compelled to warn, suddenly remembering that his idea of a fundraiser likely differed considerably from hers.

His look of horror immediately dispelled her concerns. "If I'd wanted fancy, I would have asked Ryan for help."

Her cell phone vibrated on one of the tables where she'd left it while she hung posters. She checked the number. It was her bartender, Ford. He never called her at the last minute like this. She crossed her fingers and hoped nothing was wrong.

"Excuse me," she said. "I have to take this call."

"I'm so sorry, Hannah, but I can't make it tonight," Ford said. He had a last-minute, out-of-town job interview that evening, which left her on her own.

"Don't worry about it. Good luck with the interview," she added, because she liked Ford and he needed the steady work. She wished she could afford to hire him full time, but she'd deliberately started her business out small and was a year away from being able to afford permanent staff.

"Trouble?" Dallas asked as she set her phone down.

"Not really. My bartender had to cancel, but I can manage without him."

Dallas's face brightened. "I could fill in for him, if you like."

Dallas, in a roomful of women?

She should draw up a list for him of all the things that could go wrong.

"I can't ask you to do that," she said.

"You didn't ask me. I offered. C'mon. It sounds like fun. I'll get to watch a group of women drink too much while they gamble away their life's savings."

"What wouldn't be fun about that?" she said, scrambling for a way out. "Have you ever tended bar, before?"

"No, but I've poured plenty of beer. Plus, I worked as a stripper to pay for college, so I'm used to fending off drunken women. Didn't Alayna ever tell you why she calls me Doctor Dancy Pants?"

A stripper. That was it. That was exactly what people who didn't know him would see at first glance, especially when he was wearing half-undone, casual office attire—the way he was now. But Hannah couldn't figure out if he was serious or not.

"Did you really pay for college by stripping?"

"I really did. Would you like me to demonstrate for you?"

"I'll take your word for it." She could already picture it quite fine in her head.

"It's settled, then." Dallas rubbed his hands briskly, chin up, eyes scanning the room to see what work was yet to be done. "Let me help you with those posters."

Trying to stop him once he made up his mind was like spitting on a fully engaged house fire, so she didn't try.

Once they finished with the posters, Dallas helped her rearrange the tables so they could seat six groups of four. The winners of each game would move on to the next table. The person with the most poker chips at the end of the evening won a growler of their choice of whatever beer Hannah had on tap.

She'd painted a pair of old sheets to look like bookcases—part of the speakeasy disguise—and they hung those with thumbtacks so they concealed the front window. She hung a CLOSED DUE TO NATIONAL PROHIBITION sign on the outside of the main door.

"I downloaded jazz and swing to go with the theme. You're in charge of the sound system," she said, showing him the speakers she'd mounted on either side of the bar and how to control them.

After that, she gave him a quick rundown of the taps.

"The drinks are paid for, so you don't have to worry about handling money or cards, and I'm only serving one brew—it's got a bit of a kick to it, so the servings are smaller than usual. Glasses go in the dishwasher, over here." She showed him where it was located under the bar. She plunked a tin on top of the counter. "This is for tips."

He poked at the can. "It's going to feel weird not collecting five-dollar bills in my G-string."

"Five-dollar bills?" she echoed, wide-eyed and only partly kidding. "Exactly how good were you at stripping?"

"I offered you a demonstration. If you really want to know, all you have to do is say yes."

Now that he'd planted the image of him in a G-string, she couldn't unsee it. She'd watched him strut his stuff like Mick Jagger along with a hundred or so guests at the wedding. She'd been naked with him, too—well, partially naked—but it had been dark and for the most part, she'd kept her eyes shut. Even so, she'd participated enthusiastically enough that her entire body flushed in remembrance.

But a G-string...

"Have you eaten yet?" she asked, figuring a shift in subject was in order.

"No worries. I can go grab something and be back in half an hour."

The least she could do was feed him. She'd ordered vegetable trays for the evening, but that wasn't much of a meal. "How about if you come upstairs with me and I make sandwiches for us?"

Hannah led him to the door to her upstairs apartment in the small alcove between the taproom and the brewery. Her kitchen space was a bit of a mess. She hadn't cleaned up from breakfast and lunch—she'd been busy and it hadn't seemed too bad until she'd brought a guest into it.

"This is nice," Dallas said, looking around. He wandered over to examine the bicycle chain cowboy in the corner between the bedroom and the window. "Is this one of your brother's pieces?"

"It is," she confirmed. "So is the one hanging from the ceiling downstairs in the taproom."

"It's amazing. Damon is talented."

Hannah agreed. She was proud of her older brother. He'd inspired her to follow her dream, even though she was now on her own, and helped get her started.

She opened the refrigerator and pulled out sliced corned beef, sauerkraut, swiss cheese, butter, and Thousand Island dressing. She found a jar of garlic dill pickles buried behind the milk. She stacked the sandwich fixings on the butcherblock island and got rye bread and a cutting board from one of the cupboards. She set the frying pan on the stove and began to butter the bread. "I hope you like Reuben sandwiches."

"I do."

He swung one of the stools at the island around and sat, his folded arms on the backrest and his chin on his arms, watching her quietly while she worked.

She was a good cook. Her mother, who liked to feed people, had made certain of it. But having Dallas as an audience of one didn't help her presentation skills in the least. As she grilled the sandwiches in the hot pan, the top slices of bread kept sliding off and the sauerkraut spilled out.

"Why don't you tell me about your day?" she finally suggested. Anything to get her mind off the way he watched her. Besides, she was curious.

"Do you really want to hear about it?"

She paused in the act of flipping a sandwich, her spatula in the air, surprised by the question. "Why wouldn't I?"

"I was in outpatients all day. Summer colds and angina aren't all that exciting. Most people are more interested in what comes through the emergency department."

She got the sandwiches safely back in the pan, bottom side up, without any major disasters. "Tell me why you prefer your work at the clinic. Or you could tell me why you love being a doctor so much."

Dallas eyed her with appreciation. "Most people don't notice I love it."

"Really?" How could they not? "Why else would you take up stripping to fund your degree? Wait. Let me guess." She pointed the spatula at him. "You studied medicine because the expensive education gave you an excuse to become a stripper, which is your true calling in life."

"Medical school did help me release my inner exhibitionist," he mused, a smile in his eyes. "Okay. You asked for it. I love being a doctor for lots of reasons. I like solving a mystery through diagnosis. Is that lingering cough really the beginnings of lung cancer? Or is it an allergic reaction? Can it be treated naturally, allowed to run its course, or does it require more intensive therapy? I also like getting to know my patients. Most of them fascinate me. Did you know that, when I ask how much they drink, I have to double the amount most of them give me? I only have one patient I really believe answers that question honestly and she probably shouldn't. It says a lot about her lifestyle. Or lack of a life."

"I doubt if I could answer the question at all." She transferred the sandwiches from the hot pan to two plates. "It's an occupational hazard. I do a fair bit of sampling, but I can't remember the last time I drank a whole pint."

"Don't worry about it. Beer is good for your kidneys and you're probably a decade or two away from liver disease, so carry on."

That made her laugh. She added pickles to each plate, then set Dallas's sandwich in front of him. She dragged the second stool around the corner of the island so they sat perpendicular to each other, not side by side, so they could talk more comfortably. This was nice.

"What about you? Why did you get into brewing?" he asked. "I can totally see stripping playing a role in that decision too, by the way. Alcohol raises your basal body temperature and lowers your inhibitions. Both lead to removing your clothes."

Didn't she know it.

She couldn't blame alcohol entirely for her lowered inhibitions where he was concerned, however. He'd managed to lower them all on his own—and not because he was so sexy either, although he certainly was that. It was because he'd offered her his undivided attention at a time when she'd needed it most. He'd made her feel as if she mattered to him and he cared what she thought.

The same as he was doing right now.

"I was waitressing at a bar to help put Tim through college," she said. "I was terrible at it. One of the owners took pity on me and asked if I'd like to learn how to brew beer instead. Tim was majoring in business and he needed a project for one of his courses, so we drew up a business plan together and it grew legs from there. He was going to handle the marketing while I managed operations. When he took a job with a large company in Bozeman instead, and decided he preferred a coworker to me, I didn't see any reason not to follow through with the plan—all I did was change the location from Bozeman to Grand, then rework the financing." She'd wanted to get as far away from Bozeman and Sweetheart and everything Tim-related as possible, but without leaving Montana. This was her home.

"The guy was stupid."

"He always had big dreams."

He'd relied on Hannah for follow-through, though. Even in high school. He would never have made it through college without her pushing him, either. In hindsight, now that her heart no longer hurt quite so much, she could see how he'd likely grown to resent her. She represented where he came from. Once she'd helped him get as far as she could and was no longer useful, he didn't like the reminder that he was a poor boy from Sweetheart, a small, rural town. It made her sad—not for herself, but for the teenagers they'd been. The boy she'd fallen in love with no longer existed. The man he'd become was someone she didn't know. She had no reason to make excuses for him anymore.

"His big dreams aren't what make him stupid," Dallas said. "He took his eye off the prize. There's his mistake."

She flushed. The warm way he looked at her said he believed she was the prize. He made her feel like one, too. He had from the moment they met. She'd been flattered when he introduced himself to her at the Bar-No Sweetheart Ranch, but she'd been too wrapped up in her insecurities to believe she deserved the attention he gave her. She'd convinced herself he was attracted to the fake, happy Hannah she pretended to be. That all he wanted was sex and any warm body would do.

And yet, here he was. Sitting and sharing a meal with her. Discussing their work at the end of the day. This was how things should be when two adults were attracted to each other. Every breath she drew—every glance in his direction—left her dizzy with hyperawareness. Dallas was a man, not a boy.

She wasn't a girl anymore, either.

✳

Dallas

DALLAS ADDED LIQUID soap to the hot water and washed the dishes while Hannah changed clothes. She'd cooked, so cleanup was only fair.

He had no trouble believing that she'd put her ex-boyfriend through school. The guy's dreams might be big, but starting a brewery business from scratch had apparently proven too big for him. The woman he'd left her for would undoubtedly be someone who could help him further his career, too.

What a blind, selfish bastard. He hadn't appreciated what he already had. His loss was going to be Dallas's gain.

And Dallas would never, ever, make the mistake of undervaluing Hannah.

Dishes done, he made himself comfortable on a sofa that was well past its prime but worked with the eclectic vibe of the room. She had her brother's artistic eye for design. When he compared her apartment to his house, which had been professionally decorated by an interior designer, he found his sadly lacking. Her space felt lived in whereas he used his for sleeping. Other than hanging out with Ryan and Dan, he avoided it as much as he could.

He was admiring the view of the street through a window that took up most of one wall when the bedroom door finally opened. He turned.

And he stared.

She'd knotted her long hair in a low bun at the nape of her neck. A black velvet headband encircled her forehead. Dark eyeliner and a deep red lipstick had been added for a dramatic effect. The sleeveless, black-and-silver, flapper-style evening dress clung to the curves of her hips and breasts, which he knew from personal experience were every bit as fantastic as the dress made them appear. Glittery black fringes attached to the knee-length hem exposed slim, muscular calves when she moved. Low heels with a T-strap that managed to look sexy completed the ensemble.

"My God," he breathed, because it was the only comment his overtaxed brain could churn out.

Anxiousness brought out the blue of her eyes. She smoothed her hands down her hips. "Is it too much?"

For his heart?

Definitely. It was bouncing around in his chest like a child on a backyard trampoline.

For ladies' night, however?

"I think it's spot-on. You look beautiful," he added sincerely.

She blushed in a way that suggested she wasn't used to

hearing compliments from men—one more reason her ex was a putz. A woman like Hannah should never, ever, have to wonder about her own worth.

The temptation to touch her proved too great a test for the boundaries they'd set. He crossed the room in a few steps and reached for her hand.

"Not only are you beautiful, you're amazing," he said, lacing their fingers together and giving hers a quick squeeze. "In so many ways. You run a brewery that's well on its way to success. Your business feels pretty solid. You fix your own truck—yes, I noticed it's back on the road—and judging by the taproom and your apartment, you have a good eye for design. I should also point out that you've brightened an old man's final days."

Plus, her smile was too sweet for words.

He gathered her into his arms. His palm encountered bare flesh where the open back of her dress dipped to her waist. Her hips melted against his. She tilted her chin upward, aligning her lips closer to his, and touched her fingertips to his cheek. Lust skyrocketed into his groin. The kid on the trampoline began doing backflips.

"Thank you for saying such nice things," she said.

Then, she kissed him. It started out chaste enough, just a light brush of her lips, but his mouth had a mind of its own and far different plans. His hands refused to be left out either, and two seconds after they began roaming, logical thought completely abandoned the building. She was soft in all the places he liked. She smelled fantastic, too. Like vanilla and almond butter.

Exactly the way he remembered.

God, he wanted her so much. Her fingers dug into his butt cheeks, suggesting she felt the same way. He dipped his knees slightly and hiked up the hem of her dress, running his hands up the backs of her thighs. The long fringes trickled like thin strands of silk over his wrists.

Her skin felt like silk, too. She tasted like liquid honey.

One minute more and they'd end up in her bed.

His brain rode back in on that thought. She had an event already planned for the evening and he wouldn't ruin it for her. He wasn't going to rush her again, either.

He withdrew his hands from under her dress and returned her feet to the floor.

They were both breathing heavily.

She regained her ability to speak before he did, although she kept her gaze a little south of his chin and stared at his throat. She swiped his lips with her thumb. "You have lipstick all over your mouth."

He suspected she didn't know that the way she touched him wasn't helping to tame the situation. Not at all.

"That's an occupational hazard I'm prepared to accept." She lifted her eyes, looking puzzled. "I'm your bartender tonight, remember?" he prompted, taking it as a good sign that he had to remind her. "People will be arriving any minute now."

He assessed the damage he'd done to her appearance. Despite the care he'd tried to take, she looked as if she'd been kissed. Her mouth was bare of lipstick in patches. Her eye makeup was smeared at one corner, and her hairband, tipped slightly off-kilter. A touchup was definitely in order if she didn't want people jumping to conclusions—particularly the right ones—and a knot of fear warned she likely wasn't ready for that yet.

He didn't want her to disappear from his life once again.

"I'll go unlock the front door while you do whatever it is you need to do," he said.

"Wait." She grabbed a tissue from a box on the dresser inside her bedroom door and handed it to him. A smile crinkled her eyes. "That lipstick isn't your color."

"Thanks."

He wiped his mouth and tucked the tissue in his pocket, then headed downstairs.

Chapter Eight

Hannah

"WHY IS DR. Tucker moonlighting as your bartender?" Eleanor Fitzpatrick asked Hannah.

Eleanor was a no-nonsense woman well past middle age. They were seated together on the third round of poker. Sue Anne Nylund, the gray-haired school secretary for Marion Street Grand Elementary, and Kendall McKinley, the local real estate agent who'd helped Hannah buy the building for the Grand Master Brewery, shared their table. Louis Armstrong's trumpet blared "West End Blues" from the bar, the volume comfortable for conversation while setting the tone for the evening.

So far, Eleanor was the frontrunner where winnings were concerned, leading to good-natured speculation as to a misspent youth. Hannah liked her a lot, even if she did ask intrusive questions. Eleanor, however, was only lending voice to what everyone in the room thought but didn't have enough drinks in them yet to ask. They would though. The night was young.

"Ford called at the last minute to say he couldn't make it, so Dallas offered to help out." Hannah hoped to leave it at that, but she should have known better. She'd been raised in a small rural town and she knew how to dodge and deflect when it came to speculation.

"So, Dr. Tucker was here when Ford called in sick?" Eleanor persisted.

"Dallas dropped by because he wants to use the taproom to host a fundraiser for the new free clinic the Endeavour is building. All donations are welcome, by the way," she threw in, happy to promote a worthy cause while changing the subject. Lots of rumors ran rampant in Grand, including a tidbit that suggested Posey Davies-McGregor had plenty of money to spare. A better-known fact was that Posey and Eleanor were close.

Eleanor leaned across the table and whispered, "You know, dear, you might want to pay a bit more attention. From the way he watches you, funds aren't the only thing Dr. Tucker is hoping to raise."

Sue Anne and Kendall started to laugh.

Hannah's overheated face had nothing to do with alcohol raising her basal body temperature. She knew he'd been watching her because she'd been watching him, too. The kiss they shared had already guaranteed she'd be able to focus on nothing else for the rest of the night. It was why she was drinking when normally, especially while hosting ladies' night, she'd be more... circumspect.

Circumspect.

What a great word.

"You'd make a beautiful couple. Imagine what your children would look like," Kendall mused thoughtfully once the laughter subsided. She was on her second drink. So was Hannah, so she wasn't judging. Thankfully, she'd thought to make arrangements with a taxi company for the taproom's customer home delivery service this evening because it didn't look as if she'd be able to drive.

Sue Anne weighed in with her opinion. "Test drive him first. You want to make sure he's good in bed before you start thinking about children. They'll tie you down."

Eleanor blinked. "Good heavens, Sue Anne. How could Dallas Tucker be anything but good in bed? Just look at him."

"I heard he used to be a stripper," Kendall volunteered. "Although I got that from Simone Parker so you might want to take it for what it's worth."

"Full nude or did he wear a cup? Did she say? Because a cup can be padded," Sue Anne said.

"It's not the size that matters. It's what he does with it," Eleanor cut in.

Sue Anne patted her arm. "You poor dear. If you can believe that, then you have no idea what you missed out on. Trust me. Size matters."

"Now wait just a minute," Eleanor sputtered, indignant. "My Gordon wasn't lacking in either department."

Hannah's face could start a brushfire by now. Dallas wasn't lacking in anything either, which wasn't something they needed to know. Unfortunately, she was far better at dodge and deflection than outright untruths, and if someone asked a direct question requiring an answer, she didn't think she could carry it off.

She lifted her empty glass and waved it to get Dallas's attention. Hopefully, his presence would put an end to this particular line of inquiry.

He brought over a tray of fresh drinks, distributed them to Duke Ellington's "Black and Tan Fantasy" then collected the discarded glasses with the skill of a pro. "You ladies appear to be enjoying yourselves," he remarked.

His comment was greeted with a fresh burst of laughter. Hannah took a long sip of her drink, grateful for the relaxing effects of the two she'd already downed, and refused to make eye contact.

"Is it true you used to be a stripper?" Kendall asked him, proving alcohol really did lower inhibitions.

Dallas cast a sharp look at Hannah, who wanted to crawl through the floor. Three of these tiny snifters wouldn't be nearly enough to get her through the entire evening. "She didn't hear that from me," she said quickly.

Too quickly, perhaps. Speculation puckered Eleanor's forehead, drawing one eyebrow upward. "How could Kendall have heard it from you?"

The question had everyone's attention swinging to Hannah, Dallas's included.

"Yes, Hannah, how?" he echoed. Humor danced in his hazel eyes. Or maybe the beer only made it seem as if it did.

"I…" She fumbled for an explanation but none came to mind.

He took pity and answered for her. "It's no big secret, Mrs. Fitzgerald. Hannah and I both come from Sweetheart and I know her sister. She calls me Dr. Dancy Pants."

"*Hannah* calls you Dr. Dancy Pants?" Kendall asked, wide-eyed and incredulous. She gave Hannah a thumbs-up of approval under the table.

Hannah didn't need that rumor spreading all over Grand. "No. My sister does."

"Hannah calls me 'honey' or 'darling,'" Dallas offered.

"You're fired, honey. Go home," she said.

He balanced the tray on one arm and patted her shoulder. "I'll bring over a vegetable tray for the table. You know how cranky you get when you drink on an empty stomach, babe."

It amazed her that he could participate in this conversation with such a straight face. She wished she cared as little as he did about other people's opinions.

As soon as she thought it, she knew she was wrong. He cared what people thought about the things he believed were important. He cared a great deal about the opinions of the nursing home residents and staff, in fact. They loved him for it, too. Eleanor, Sue Anne, and Kendall were being equally charmed at this very moment.

Meanwhile Hannah, for her part, couldn't honestly claim to be immune. The buzzing in her head wasn't entirely due to the drinks she'd consumed.

It had begun earlier, upstairs, when she'd kissed him.

She'd kissed him the night of the wedding, too.

She'd known what would happen the moment he invited her to go for a walk. He was a romantic. A gentleman. He insisted she wear his jacket for warmth. He told her silly jokes to make her laugh. He gave her his arm because her shoes weren't meant for long walks in the dark on gravel pathways, and noticed when they became uncomfortable. She wasn't beautiful like Alayna, or smart like Claire, and yet this gorgeous man, with the tangle of dark curls and the beautiful eyes, who thought nothing of performing a barely decent dance routine for two hundred wedding guests, made her feel special.

She'd wanted him so much that a bolder, less inhibited, Hannah emerged.

Then, the next day, reality returned. Her life was a mess. Her heart had only recently been broken and hadn't yet healed. All Bold Hannah had done was complicate things.

But now, things were different. Her life was on a new track. The Grand Master Brewery was off to a great start.

Best of all, her heart no longer hurt.

She was ready to move on. Dallas would be a great place to start.

Sue Anne's eyes tracked him all the way to the bar. Blood pulsed against the top of Hannah's skull. She shot back half of her snifter and waited in fear for Sue Anne to ask her if she knew whether or not he wore a cup. Heat licked the underside of her belly. She had no idea, but if he did wear one, there'd be no reason to pad it.

Sue Anne sighed. "That is one fine man. If I were twenty years younger, I'd pad his cup with twenties."

Eleanor picked up the card deck, cut it, and shuffled with a skill that didn't bode well for the rest of the table. "I think you meant to say forty years younger. But then, math skills are the first to go." She smiled brightly. "Okay, ladies. Let's get down to business."

Luckily, Hannah had no real money on the line because, for the remainder of the evening, her head wasn't at all in the game. She lost every card hand for the rest of the evening.

At ten o'clock, husbands, boyfriends, and teenaged children with driver's licenses began arriving to collect those who'd arranged for their own transportation. Eleanor, armed with her six-pack of winnings, accepted a lift from a neighbor. Dallas helped Kendall and Sue Anne into one of the cabs Hannah had booked.

He closed the taproom door behind the last departing guest and flipped the dead bolt into position. Bessie Smith belted out "St. Louis Blues." He picked up a half-empty glass someone had left on a table.

"How much alcohol is in this beer, anyway?" he asked,

holding the thick cocoa brew to the light and examining it as if it might somehow talk.

Hannah bounced her bare heels off the rung of her stool. She'd discarded her shoes at some point—she wasn't sure when. "Twelf percent." That didn't sound right. She tried again. "Twelve."

There. That was better.

"*Twelve?*" Dallas goggled at her.

"I aged it in Canadian whiskey barrels to get the maple flavor," she explained, defensive. "I told everyone that."

"Yes, but did everyone understand that the beer soaks up alcohol as well as the flavor?"

"That's plain common sense."

For some reason, he seemed to think that answer was funny. "Sure it is—if you're a brew master. Since when is Canadian whiskey maple-flavored, anyway?"

"The whiskey isn't. The barrels it comes in are made of maple wood." She put her finger to her lips. "But my secret—don't tell anyone—is that I also add maple syrup to the wort after it boils. The fermented sh-sh-sh-sugar is what really bumps up the alcohol content."

"Your secret is safe with me. Judging by the number of glasses I filled, I'd say your recipe is a resounding success." He began clearing tables.

Hannah hopped off the stool, then grabbed the edge of the table when the floor spun upward to meet her. "You don't have to stick around. I can clean up."

Dallas lifted her by the elbows and deposited her back on the stool she'd vacated. "How about you sit right there and supervise me instead, boss lady. I have fifty-six dollars in tips to work off."

"And the drinks were already paid for… Imagine how much you could have made if you'd worn a G-string," Hannah marveled.

"You're cute when you're drunk."

"I'm not drunk." She thought for a second. "Yes I am. But only a little."

"It doesn't matter. You're cute when you're sober, too."

"Thank you. Can I tell you another secret?"

"You can tell me anything you like. I promise I'll keep it to myself."

Bold Hannah came out—the one who'd played milk-maid in a stable with him. "Kissing you is good. Really, really good. But you are *great* in bed. In fact, sex with you is the best I've ever had."

The sound that came out of him was a cross between a strangled laugh and a groan. "That's probably a secret you're going to regret telling me later, but thank you. I feel the same way about sex with you."

Bold Hannah was pleased. "Want to try it again?"

"The answer to that is a resounding yes, but I'm sensing a pattern. Why don't we shake things up a little and try it without the influence of alcohol?"

Everyday Hannah was going to be horribly embarrassed

by this conversation tomorrow, but right now, she was too disappointed to care. She'd needed a few drinks in order to bring Bold Hannah out and it turned out she'd wasted her time. "Are you turning me down?"

"God, no. Well, yes," he amended. "But only for to-night—and think of it more as a deferral, because it's definitely not a rejection. I'd like to take you out to dinner first."

She perked up. "As in a date?"

"Exactly. A date," he confirmed. "There'll be dancing involved, too. How about Sunday, since you work every evening before then?"

"Not until after my visit with Marsh, though." Neither Bold nor Everyday Hannah was giving that up.

"Even better—why don't I pick you up early, we'll visit Marsh together, then go out to dinner?"

"He'd love that. He thinks we make a cute couple," she volunteered. Both Hannahs slapped their mental foreheads. *Shut up, Stupid Hannah.*

"He does, does he?" Dallas finished loading the dish-washer. He snapped the door closed and turned it on. "There. All done."

He was fast and efficient. She hadn't even noticed him dispose of the empty food trays.

"Thank you for helping out this evening," she said.

Dallas smiled at her in a way that made her toes curl. "The pleasure was mine."

He stooped to kiss her cheek, which wasn't satisfying at all. She wanted another kiss like the one they'd shared earlier. She draped her arms on his shoulders and clasped her fingers behind his neck.

"Sunday, Hannah," he said firmly, and disentangled himself. "Sleep well. And don't forget to lock up behind me."

✳

Dallas

SEX WITH YOU is the best I've ever had.

The whole drive home, Dallas couldn't stop grinning. Hannah might have had a few drinks, but only enough to free up her filter and not enough for him to worry about leaving her alone to lock up. The kiss they'd shared had happened before the drinking began, too, and it gave him a good idea of where things between them really stood.

She believed she'd been playing a role when they first met. He thought the exact opposite was true—that she'd been stifled by her ex since she was a teenager and had let the real Hannah loose for the first time at the wedding. He'd caught another glimpse of that Hannah tonight, over the sandwiches they'd shared, then again when they kissed, but she'd still had to work up the courage to invite him upstairs at the end of the night. It was why he'd decided it was a bad idea to stay. There weren't going to be any regrets the next morning, this time. Not if he had any say.

Meanwhile, even though he knew he wasn't suffering from priapism—a true erectile dysfunction—the constant up-and-down state she'd left him in since last October was uncomfortable, to say the least. Knowing it wasn't going to kill him didn't help.

Ryan and Dan were in the common room waiting for him when he walked through the front door shortly before midnight. Dan's leg was healing nicely, although he had it propped on one of the leather sofas so he'd likely overdone it that day. Dallas flopped on the sofa closest to him and yawned.

"Hard day at the hospital?" Ryan asked from the chair facing him.

"Terrible," Dallas lied. "Steady stream of patients. One disaster after another."

His friends looked at each other and laughed.

"I stopped by outpatients at five o'clock to ask you about a change the builders want to make in the free clinic's design and they told me you'd already left for the day," Ryan said. "You missed our Wednesday night briefing session, too. You're supposed to have a reminder programmed into your phone." He sniffed. "Why do you smell like beer?"

Damn. He'd forgotten all about their weekly meeting. Now he'd have to file a written report because Ryan took these things seriously. It was just one more reason why Dallas hated money so much. "I stopped at the Grand Master Brewery to discuss using it as a venue for the clinic's fundraiser and ended up staying for a few games of chess and a beer."

"Wasn't this supposed to be ladies' night at the taproom? Jazz has gone once or twice when things were quiet at the smoke jumper base and I was working," Dan said.

"I guess that explains why I was the only man there."

"You've been spending a lot of time at the brewery over the past few weeks," Ryan remarked. He sounded casual enough, but he didn't fool Dallas. "Should we be worried? Stress getting to you?"

"Absolutely," Dallas said. "I drink too much and I've developed a substance abuse problem, too. I've been stealing narcotics from the hospital."

"You tend to be a stressor, not a stressee, and I doubt if your alcohol and substance abuse issues are the reason you hang out at the taproom," Dan said. "Hannah Brand is pretty."

The penny dropped. Ryan's gaze took on the glint of a raptor focused on prey. "She is. She's also the girl you met at your friend's wedding whose boyfriend is now out of the picture, isn't she?"

"The one you thought might be after Dallas's money?" Dan asked. "Hannah doesn't really seem like the type." He settled in as if preparing to watch a drama unfold.

"All women are the type," Ryan said.

Dallas hadn't forgotten that Ryan believed Hannah used him as an excuse to break up with her ex-boyfriend for good. She'd pretty much confirmed it, so he wasn't wrong. But that was all past history now. They had a date lined up for Sunday. He didn't want his friends puncturing his fantastic mood, no matter how good their intentions might be. Ryan really needed to get past his childhood issues.

"I have a vaccine clinic for babies in the morning so I need to get some sleep. You wouldn't believe how worked up parents get if you're careless with a needle," Dallas said.

"Just a minute." Ryan waved for him to stay seated. "We've been discussing the possibility of a week-long camping trip to explore the ranch. Neither of you has really taken the time to see it all."

A *week*?

Dallas pointed out the obvious. "Dan and I can't just walk away from our jobs. I say we don't micromanage the hired hands. There's over one hundred and fifteen thousand acres of land we'd have to cover."

That equaled one hundred and eighty square miles and significant portions of neighboring counties. Not to mention three thousand cows, eight hundred heifers, and one hundred and fifty range bulls. They'd recently begun adding Tennessee Walker horses to the mix, because why not. Annual crop yields consisted of twenty-five thousand tons of alfalfa hay and seven hundred thousand bushels of wheat and barley. One hundred acres of cleared land contained an airbase with three runways and hangar facilities, a smoke-jumper base, and the free clinic. Next summer the main ranch in Grand would support a group home for at-risk youth—or, as Dallas liked to refer to them, teenagers.

The extent of their inheritance boggled the mind. And that was before factoring in all the money, which really, paid the Endeavour's major expenses. Ranching at this scale wasn't for the poor, fainthearted, or anyone lacking serious commitment. That was why they'd left management up to Ryan. He excelled at it.

"I know you're both busy." Ryan didn't come right out and say it, but the side-eye he gave Dan included his off-duty relationship with Jazz. Dan shrugged it off with the smile of a man who had everything he wanted in life. "But think of it as a corporate retreat," Ryan continued.

"Really? What's our corporate goal?" Dallas asked.

Ryan grinned. "Fly-fishing."

Dallas liked fly-fishing. "What week are we talking about?"

"How about next weekend?"

Dallas was torn. Things were going okay with Hannah, but they were by no means a done deal. He was a little surprised that Dan didn't argue either, because Jazz's contract would soon be up and they didn't have the logistics of their relationship ironed out yet. Thanks to prior commitments they'd be looking at a long-distance romance for the foreseeable future, so they spent every spare moment together.

The fact that Dan hadn't argued meant this trip was important to Ryan. A guys' weekend was something they'd done every few years since they'd graduated from college. The last was a trip to Flathead Lake three, maybe four years ago, while Dallas was finishing his residency, so they were past due.

Come to think of it, Ryan looked like he might be the one suffering from stress. Faint lines at the corners of his eyes and a touch of premature gray at his temples hadn't been there back in January when they'd begun holding these meetings. Plus, he'd been moody for weeks. More so than usual. Guilt pinched at Dallas. He'd been happy to let Ryan make all of the Endeavour's business decisions. A little too happy, perhaps.

Since he had to be careful not to rush Hannah, and he wasn't the most patient of guys, this trip would provide an opportunity to give her some distance while taking care of his obligations to the Endeavour Ranch team. Ryan—Dan, too—deserved some of his time.

Plus, he really liked fly-fishing.

"A corporate retreat sounds like a great idea," he said.

Chapter Nine

Hannah

BY SATURDAY, HANNAH was ready to tell Dallas she was sick and cancel their date. They hadn't spoken since Wednesday night, when she'd made a complete fool of herself, and there was a distinct possibility that he now had regrets.

She'd told him he was great in bed. That it was the best sex she'd ever had. She alternated between burning with mortification and the ice-cold chill of horror whenever she recalled it. She'd thrown herself at him in precisely the same manner Simone had. She made a mental note to be especially kind to Simone the next time she saw her.

By Sunday, however, rather than cancel, she'd decided to be an adult and own her behavior. She'd gone on exactly one date in her adult life and that was coffee with Levi, which could best be considered a test run, because there hadn't been any sparks. There were sparks with Dallas. Plenty of them. She could be fun without being drunk and she'd prove it to him—to herself, too. She had to give up the whole "sex leads to marriage" mentality she'd had since she was fifteen. Women even voted, these days.

Deciding what to wear had taken her hours—she didn't know what he had planned—so she went with a flared, sleeveless jersey dress in a bright floral print with pink cowgirl boots and a light denim jacket. She'd pinned her hair in a messy updo and even wore makeup. A brief moment of terror had her worrying she'd underdressed for a date with a billionaire, but most of the time Dallas couldn't seem to remember he was rich, and since they were kicking the date off with a trip to the Grand Home for Special Care, it seemed highly unlikely.

Dallas texted to say he'd pick her up at two o'clock and she waited for him on the street so he wouldn't have to park. Guests had to walk through the brewery to get to her apartment and the layout wasn't ideal, which was the lone drawback to her living arrangement.

The car that pulled up to the curb had her reassessing whether or not he knew he was rich. She'd been on the lookout for his Jeep Cherokee. Instead, he drove an aggressive black Mercedes AMG that looked as if it ran on raw meat rather than gas.

He hopped out of the car to open her door. His casual outfit of jeans, dress shirt, navy sports jacket, and Chelsea boots relieved her. He'd gotten a haircut, too. He'd left it longer on top and the breeze tousled the black curls, but the sides had been somewhat tamed. The light growth of dark stubble that shadowed his chin and jaw suggested he'd shaved late last night and couldn't be bothered to repeat the process again this morning. Overall, he took an absent-minded approach to his appearance that reinforced the whole "decadent god" theme he had running, not "billionaire." He smelled wonderful, too. She suspected Tom Ford. She'd bought one of the colognes for her brother for Christmas as a thank you for helping her get her business up and running. She couldn't see Dallas buying it for himself, however, and somehow, she didn't think one of his brothers had bought it. A flutter of jealousy tapped at her ribs. She ignored it because they both had past lives. It wasn't his fault that his was by far the more interesting one.

"You look beautiful," he said.

"Thank you. I like your haircut. Nice car," she added, babbling, because otherwise, she'd simply stand there and stare at him. He was beautiful, too. Very much so.

He leaned on the passenger door while she ducked under his arm and made a valiant attempt to keep her short skirt from riding up in the back as she scrambled into the plush leather seat. Why were sports cars always so awkwardly low?

He shifted his attention from her legs to her face. Humor turned his hazel eyes golden. "The car belongs to Ryan. I like it because it looks like a character in a Batman movie."

"Bane," Hannah said, nodding. "I can see that." It made sense to her that Dallas would choose a car based on how it reminded him of the villain from a superhero movie rather than in an attempt to impress her. "Out of curiosity—do you know what an Amex black card is?"

"You mean my credit card? Ryan gave it to me."

That explained that.

When they arrived at the nursing home, Dallas insisted she wait while he opened the door. "Marsh will be watching and I can't have him think I don't know how to treat a lady," he said, taking her hand.

He knew how to make a girl feel like a lady, all right. No worries about that.

"Well, don't you two look swanky," Marsh drawled when they entered his room. "I see you made peace with your barber," he added, addressing Dallas, then coughed into his sleeve.

"Afraid not. She can't be trusted near my throat with sharp instruments, anymore. I had to find a new one in Forsyth. Now let's get you into your chair. We're heading down to the lounge," Dallas informed him.

Hannah loved listening to the back and forth between the two men. Marsh smiled more than he had when she first met him. He stayed awake longer, too. But he was losing weight and he couldn't seem to catch his breath when he spoke. She didn't like the sound of his cough, either.

Marsh was a two-person transfer, and Dallas wouldn't allow Hannah to help because she hadn't had training, so they called for one of the nursing assistants. By the time they arrived in the lounge, a small group of residents had heard

Dallas was visiting and already gathered.

Hannah had assumed they were going to play with the virtual reality headsets. Instead, Dallas turned on the music. Tim McGraw began to croon.

"I promised to take Hannah dancing," he said to the room, which included a few of the staff members now, too. "What do you think? Want to place bets as to whether or not she can manage a one-step?" His smile grew wicked. "Because I already know she's got two left feet when it comes to line dancing."

She'd never live down that YouTube video of her flashing her panties.

"The problem's got to be you, Dr. Dallie. She's too pretty to be a bad dancer," the Santa Claus lookalike said.

"Hold on to that thought, Rudy," Dallas replied, already moving his shoulders and hips in time to the music. He beckoned to Hannah. A glint of challenge lurked in his eyes.

She slipped her fingers into his and returned his smile sweetly. He knew she could dance. They'd danced together before. This was all in good fun and she loved helping him keep the seniors entertained. "I'll try to keep up, Dr. Dancy Pants," she said.

He glided her around the room, his knees nudging her whenever a change in direction was called for. He spun her by the hand on every fourth step so that her short skirt twirled out in a colorful circle. When the song ended, he pulled her close to his chest for a beat, then bent her over his thigh so that her hair skimmed the floor to the enthusiastic applause from their audience.

He whispered in her ear as he set her back on her feet. "See if you can get Rudy to dance. The exercise will do him good. But he might be a little unsteady without his walker, so hang onto him. I'm going to take Bernice for a spin around the floor in her wheelchair."

If Hannah hadn't already been attracted to him, that would have been enough to tip the scales in his favor. Any man who took the time to be so kind to seniors would make her heart flutter. Dallas made it stampede.

Rudy, it turned out, was an excellent dancer.

"Hands above the waist," Dallas warned him, shaking a finger.

"She's a foot taller than me. How am I supposed to do that?" Rudy, whose hands were already steady at her waist, complained. He winked at her and she laughed.

The rest of the afternoon, she had so much fun. Marsh wasn't interested in dancing from a wheelchair—he was too dignified for that—but he enjoyed watching her dance with Dallas.

They danced a few more times together, and got the staff involved too, before Dallas glanced at his watch. "Sorry everyone, but we've got to be going. We have dinner reservations for seven o'clock."

"It's barely four," someone protested.

"Yes, but the restaurant isn't in Grand."

Now he had Hannah's attention, too. Where were they going that it would take them three hours to get there?

They returned Marsh to his room, with Hannah pushing his wheelchair while he chatted with Dallas, then left him seated by the window, half asleep. The late summer sun beat at them as they crossed the parking lot to the car. Dallas carried his jacket slung over his shoulder.

"Where is this restaurant?" Hannah asked.

"You'll see."

They followed the I-94 along the Yellowstone River for twenty-five minutes until they reached the turnoff for Forsyth. Dallas parked the AMG at a curb near the high school with a rather shocking disregard for its safety, given his opinion of the neighborhood where she lived and this wasn't much different. Music rumbled through the air. It appeared to originate a few blocks to their left.

"There's a street dance tonight," he said, sounding almost apologetic, which fired her curiosity. "A local band is playing. I thought we'd check it out for a few hours, then have dinner at the Dirty Glass Alehouse."

The local band turned out to be a group of high school seniors who hadn't yet decided what they wanted to be when they grew up. Their playlist featured everything from Mongolian death metal to a Disturbed-inspired interpretation of Johnny Cash. They were talented, although somewhat uncertain about their musical career path in life. The enthusiastic bass from the woofers pounded at the chest in a way that staved off any potential need for defibrillation. Even though the band was at the far end of the street, speakers mounted on the sides of buildings guaranteed ruptured eardrums for all.

Dallas took her hand so they couldn't be swept apart by the group of gyrating teenagers working their way up the street. "Not quite what I envisioned when I was invited to this," he said. "While I'm a huge fan of death metal personally, my headbanging days are long behind me. It can cause brain damage, not to mention what repeated exposure to loud music does to your hearing, so professionally, I'm obliged to be somewhat opposed."

He'd been invited. That explained why he'd sounded so apologetic—although he had no need to worry. She thought it was sweet that he followed through on his commitments. She clung to his hand, half afraid to let go for fear he'd get wrapped up on the music and forget she was with him. She had no idea how he kept everything straight.

"You have the weirdest interests," she said.

"Says the woman who brews maple beer." He laced his fingers through hers and tugged her out of the path of two oncoming men carrying cans of soda, although judging by the fumes, the labels were lying. "I'm sensing this isn't your thing."

"It's too soon to say. I can't remember the last time I went to a night club, let alone a street dance that features… what is this? Death metal folk country?"

"No idea. We'll give it a few more minutes. If you still aren't enjoying yourself by the time we reach the end of the street, we'll move on to dinner. The band invited me out of a sense of obligation because I agreed to sponsor the event, not a burning desire to have me attend. They won't mind if we take off."

Hannah's heart melted. Dallas had sponsored a street dance for a group of high school students simply because he was asked. That had to be the sweetest, most generous thing she'd ever heard. The crowd and the music dissipated into little more than white noise.

"I love everything about this," she said sincerely. "I say we close the joint down."

His laugh could be seen in his eyes. "Let's not get all crazy. Hearing loss is permanent and the danger is real."

They stayed for an hour. When the band took a break, Dallas introduced her to them and it was immediately apparent the lead singer had a serious case of hero worship for him that was beyond cute. She also learned the music they played was called country death. Who knew there was such a thing?

By the time they reached the restaurant, the boys weren't the only ones who were hero worshipping Dallas. Hannah, too, thought he was amazing. So much so, in fact, that caution stepped in to give her a stern talking to and remind her of a few things. She'd been single for less than a year, and while it was okay to enter into an adult relationship with

Dallas, she might want to dial back on the infatuation a bit and refocus more on the fun.

✳

Dallas

DALLAS FOLLOWED HANNAH and the waitress to a quiet booth at the back of what had once been a pub but was now a five-star restaurant, according to Yelp.

He didn't especially care about its rating as long as the food was good and it didn't play death metal. Country music either, for that matter. He'd never listen to Johnny Cash or Waylon Jennings the same way again. Thank God Hannah was such a good sport.

She looked so pretty, too. He liked the brightly patterned clothes she seemed to prefer. Pediatric nurses wore the same cheerful colors and bold patterns because their little patients were attracted to them, but while he'd been accused more than once of being a big kid, he felt fairly certain that her choice of clothing wasn't what attracted him to her.

He'd be the first to admit that he wasn't always a good date. He'd been told that more than once, too. He felt guilty for bringing her to a street dance for their first date. He'd wanted to do something special for her, but he'd hated to disappoint the kids, and this was the only way he could figure out how to work everything in. The visit to the nursing home, on the other hand, had been a win from the start because she'd intended to go anyway, and all it meant was that he got to pick her up early and spend extra time with her.

Hannah smiled up at him as he waited while she slid into her seat. The candlelight caught blue eyes that sparkled with mischief. "You should bring the Screaming Wolverines to the nursing home for one of their activity hours. They'd make an excellent backup in case any pacemakers malfunctioned."

"They would. We could also add them to the code blue team at the hospital. Then we wouldn't have to worry about keeping the defibrillators charged, either." He took his own seat across from her. "Thank you for being such a great sport."

"There's no need to thank me. I'm having a good time."

She meant it.

Relief tempered some of the guilt and lifted a weight from his shoulders. They ordered steaks, then talked about the fundraiser he had yet to put any real thought into.

"I have no idea what's involved in fundraising," he admitted. "I've always avoided anything even remotely related, although I get that it's necessary. Kind of like having chicken pox when you're a kid. Don't hospitals usually hire people for things like that?"

Hannah studied him across the table. "You don't have time for it, do you? Would you like me to take care of it for you?"

"You'd do that?" He sounded almost as pathetically grateful as he felt. "I don't want to impose. You have a business to run."

"Luckily for you, it's part of my business. If you have to hire someone to organize it for you, it might as well be me." Her brow puckered in thought. "I'll donate my fee and write it off as a tax deduction. You'll have to pay the expenses for the event, though. I'm not in a position to carry those yet, although I hope to be, in a few years."

"You're a far better business person than I am," he said. "If someone hadn't given me money, I'd still be running a small country practice in Sweetheart."

"Is that what you'd rather be doing?"

"It was at first. I miss my patients. Most of them have known me since I was a kid and I liked that I was giving back to my community. But I still get to help people, and now I have the money to do even more, so I have no reason to complain," he said. He tried not to, at least.

"Most people don't complain about having too much money."

"Most people don't have Ryan O'Connell managing it for them."

That brought out another one of her pretty smiles. The waitress delivered their meals, interrupting the conversation. Hannah toyed with her plate, shifting it around the table.

"About the other night. I should apologize," she finally

said.

Dallas looked up from his steak. "What for?"

"I had way too much to drink."

"Did you wake up naked with a hangover the size of Montana and a bull's-eye tattooed on one of your glutes?"

Her lips curved up at the corners. "I don't think so."

"Then you didn't have *way* too much to drink. Just a *little* too much. Trust me on that. I can show you my tattoo so you can see the difference."

"You do not have a tattoo of a bull's-eye on one of your 'glutes,'" Hannah said. "I'd have noticed." She blushed as she said it. She was such fun to tease.

"You must not have been paying close enough attention," he said.

"I paid attention."

The pink on her cheeks deepened until it matched the hue of her boots, but her gaze connected with his, and gamely, didn't waver. He nearly dropped his fork when he realized she was flirting with him.

"Excuse me, Dr. Tucker," a pleasant voice interrupted. "I happened to notice you when I walked in and thought I'd say hello."

Adriana Gallant. The Energizer Bunny of television tabloid reporters.

Approaching her mid-forties, but able to pass for ten years younger, she wore her dark hair in a smooth knot and sported a neutral suit on a body the camera would love.

Dallas's lungs squeezed together in prayer that she was in Forsyth because she was a huge country death music fan. He muttered "Hi," before she zeroed in on Hannah.

"You must be Hannah Brand, the owner of the Grand Master Brewery." Hannah shook the hand she was offered, a dazed look in her eyes. How Adriana found out Hannah's name was a mystery to Dallas. Her research abilities were likely why she was such a terrifying reporter. "What's it like to be dating one of the hottest bachelors in Grand?"

"I…" Hannah looked to Dallas for help.

"She's so excited, she's speechless," Dallas said.

"We never got a chance to finish our interview at the Endeavour open house," Adriana continued, making it clear that Hannah wasn't of interest to her, which was not a good sign. "I hoped I might be able to ask you a few more questions."

"We're in the middle of dinner."

"I'll only take a minute of your time. Is it true Ryan O'Connell was born in Chicago?"

"Not that I'm aware of," Dallas said. He longed to tell her to shove off, but the question about Ryan's early years raised a concern. He and Dan protected their friend's privacy as best they could and it might be best to nip this line of questioning in the bud.

"Is it also true the three of you were arrested for stealing a police car in college? And that's how you met Judge Ian Palmeter?"

"I thought those records were sealed," he said lightly.

Their brief life of crime wasn't exactly a secret, but it wasn't something many people knew about, either. As sheriff, Dan wasn't inclined to brag about it—although his issue was more with drinking and driving than heisting a police vehicle. The officer had left his keys in it. And as for Ryan…

"Why would the records be sealed?" Adriana asked, her eyes sharp, and Dallas knew he'd made a mistake by bringing that up. Sealed records protected people with something important to hide—like an identity that was changed through the witness protection program. Drunk college boys who stole police cars, not so much.

"Isn't that what happens after a judge dismisses charges?" he asked, all innocence. "Anyway, yes. That's how we met Judge Palmeter."

"And the three of you kept in touch with him all these years?"

No. Only Ryan had. He started to sweat. "You make it sound weird."

"I'm bored, baby," Hannah interrupted. She had her cheek propped on her hand and gave every indication of having recovered from her vocal paralysis of a few moments ago. She leaned toward him, dismissing Adriana completely with the angle of her head, and tracked an intimate finger up and down the forearm he'd rested on the table. Her petulant tone matched her pout. "You promised me we could spend the rest of the evening at the casino. Do you think the Lucky Lil has a high roller suite like they do at the casinos in Las Vegas?"

She was so, so adorable. He was going to kiss her the first chance he got.

"There's only one way to find out, kitten." He dropped his napkin next to his unfinished meal. "I'm sorry, Ms. Gallant, but you'll have to set up an interview through the ranch if you have any more questions. We have other plans for tonight."

He signaled to the waitress that he'd like the check. There wasn't much Adriana could say other than wish them a pleasant evening.

They emerged on the street to the blare of an old Dolly Parton song rendered almost unrecognizable by the band's cover of it. The night air had a bite to it now that the wide yellow edge of the moon peeped over the Badlands somewhere off to the northeast.

"Kitten?" Hannah said, linking her arm though his as they walked. Her hand warmed the bend of his elbow.

"Baby?" Dallas replied, raising his eyebrows.

The flickering streetlight danced in her eyes. "I was going for forties moll.'"

"Mission accomplished. Although you could have gone for twenty-first-century date being ignored and been equally successful."

"Forties moll seemed like a more interesting role."

Not to him. He liked the sound of twenty-first-century date just fine. He didn't intend for her to be ignored any longer this evening, though. From now on, she had his full attention.

"Did you really want to go to the casino?" he asked.

"No. I've had enough of crowds and loud music and we didn't get to eat our dinner. Why don't we go to my place, order a pizza, and watch a movie?"

"I don't know… Do I get to sample your maple beer?"

The pink was back in her cheeks. "If that's what you'd like to sample."

That touch of pink said she was flirting with him again. That she was making a real attempt to be bold. It reminded him of something she'd said—that when they first met, she'd tried to be something she wasn't. He didn't believe it. Hannah was sweet, she was funny, and with a little encouragement, she was also adventurous. She'd spent years with a man who'd done his best to crush the uniqueness out of her and mold her into someone better suited to him.

Dallas liked her exactly the way she was.

The desire to kiss her returned, magnified by about a million. He stopped abruptly, right there on the sidewalk, and cupped her face in his hands, forcing the two teenagers bopping their heads behind them to the beat of country death to part ways like the Yellowstone flowing around a large rock. He covered her mouth with his, tasting sweetness and promise, then inhaled deeply as he released her. A hint of a floral perfume and the fresh scent of the outdoors hung on the air. Her eyes were soft and wide.

"I'll take whatever's on tap," he said.

Chapter Ten

Dallas

H E PARKED IN the lot behind the brewery, mainly because he was curious to see if the donation he'd made to the town had gone toward having the light pole repaired as he'd requested.

"It's lit up like the county morgue back here," he commented, happy to see it. The new lighting had likely cut down on the drug deals so the rims on Ryan's AMG should be safe, too.

"Isn't it great? Now I can fix my truck at three in the morning. No more cutting into my workday," Hannah enthused as she unlocked the back door to the brewery.

Wait. What?

No amount of lighting was going to make that a wise proposition.

But his brain got tripped up on a plausibility study of pheromones he'd read, because a whiff of her warm, unique, incredibly feminine scent lent it more weight, and before he could drag his head out of its tailspin, she had the brewery door open and was already inside.

She flipped a switch on the wall. The overhead fluorescents flickered a few times in protest, then sullenly glared, as if annoyed at being disturbed. The aroma of fermenting barley wasn't as strong as he'd expected, no doubt because it vented through an air exchanger to the parking lot. Steel tanks stretched to the ceiling. Clear plastic hoses either hung on wall hooks or crisscrossed the concrete floor. The overall impression he got was one of sterility. He could perform day surgery in here.

"You run this all by yourself?" he asked, impressed enough with her setup to temporarily set aside his issues with her vehicle maintenance schedule and the results of that pheromone study for later. "How does it all work?"

She gave him a quick rundown, explaining how she created the wort recipe from the original malt, boiled and fermented it, then let it rest before filtering and kegging. "My mom is a good cook," she said. "I think that's why I like experimenting with the recipes so much."

She checked several of the tanks' gauges and fussed with one of the hoses. She'd begun to kill time, leading Dallas to suspect she might be developing second thoughts as to how their evening would end. If so, that was fine. This was only their first real date, after all. There'd be plenty more. He had Marsh and Rudy onboard.

Finally, they exited the brewery and entered the passage that led to the taproom and the stairwell to her apartment.

He cast around for a way to recapture the fun they'd been having, to make the evening unique, taking it as a personal challenge.

"How do you feel about ordering gyros with tahini sauce instead of pizza?" he asked as they climbed the stairs.

"Can you really order something like that in Grand?"

She thought he was joking. Twin blue irises ringed with traces of honey telegraphed her skepticism. He pulled out his phone. "Of course not. I'll have it flown in from LA on the ranch's private jet," he said, then laughed at the expression on her face. "Kidding. There's a Middle Eastern restaurant next to the hotel that delivers for slightly less than the cost of a private jet."

"I'm not sure whether you're serious about the gyros or not, but if you are, then I'm willing to give them a try."

He had the number programmed into his phone. He gave the restaurant the brewery's street address and asked them to call when they arrived with the delivery. He'd meet them at the front door so they didn't have to find the private entrance. When he disconnected the call, however, Hannah had her nose crinkled up.

"It's too late to change your mind. The order's already been placed," he said, shoving his phone in his jacket pocket. "I'll just have to eat your share."

Her brow cleared. They reached the top of the stairs and entered her kitchen. She'd left the light on over the kitchen stove. The only other light filtered into the room from the street through the enormous living room windows.

"I was wondering what a good beer pairing for gyros and tahini sauce might be," she said, and he relaxed.

"You should be more worried about what show we're going to watch. I'll warn you up front—medical dramas are a bad bet with me. I'm hypercritical."

She waved off his warning. "I already have a movie in mind. You're going to love it."

"I admire your confidence. What if I've already seen it?"

"Doesn't matter. If you're really a fan, it's one of those movies you won't mind watching twice."

Now she had his attention. "What makes you think I might be a fan?"

"Your taste in cars." She kicked off her pink boots by the door and took off her jacket, leaving her slender arms and legs bare. She had pretty feet. He remembered them quite well. Every inch of her, in fact. Tonight, her delicate toes were tipped in hot pink. The short skirt of her bright dress flared around her toned thighs as she hung both of their jackets on hooks, setting his thoughts into a whirlwind of lust. "Is the attraction strictly Tom Hardy or are you a Gal Gadot fan, too?"

Tom Hardy played Bane. He was officially in love with her for knowing that fact.

He clipped his brain on its leash. "Gal Gadot is pretty enough, but Tom Hardy is someone I'd turn for," he said, enjoying the conversation immensely.

It seemed she did, too. "Fair enough. I'd turn for Gal Gadot, so I understand."

"I just had a mental image of you and Wonder Woman together, and now my life is complete."

"Really? We have so much in common. My mental image of you and Tom Hardy makes my life complete, too," she said.

They'd moved into the living room as they spoke. The soft lighting loved her, upping her kissable quotient, but if he started, he wasn't sure he could stop. Then the restaurant would have made a delivery across town for no reason, they'd be annoyed, and he'd have to explain to Dan and Ryan why he tipped them an extra few hundred dollars the next time they ate there.

He picked up the TV remote from the arm of the sofa and tossed it to her. "How about if I watch for the delivery guy while you find the movie."

They ate the gyros in front of the TV, settling in to watch the movie with Hannah leaning against the armrest on one side of the sofa and Dallas on the other. She tucked her feet between the sofa's back and its cushions while he propped his legs over hers with his feet on her lap.

The movie turned out to be better than expected, based on reviews. That might have had as much to do with the company as the movie itself.

"Would you turn for Chris Pine, too?" Hannah asked when the credits rolled at the end. She wriggled her toes against his hip.

He returned the favor by tickling her ribs with his, making her squeal and squirm away, and almost upending her in the process. He swung his feet to the floor and then picked up both of hers, holding them prisoner on the tops of his thighs. He took one of her heels in his hand, pressed his thumb against the sole of her foot, and began to massage. A slight intake of breath, then a small sigh of pleasure, told him he'd made the right move.

"That depends," he said, keeping up the conversation. "Are we talking about Chris Pine as himself, as Steve Trevor, or James Tiberius Kirk?"

"Wow. I had no idea you were such a geek."

"Look who's calling the kettle black, Diana Prince."

They were both quiet for a few moments. He focused on massaging her foot, although he could feel how intently she watched him from her prone position against the arm of the sofa.

"This is nice," she said, then allowed a few more seconds to tick by before adding, "You're a good date, Dallas."

Something about the way she said it convinced him that country boys from small rural towns shouldn't be allowed to date girls until their thirties, at least. Not before they learned how to treat them right.

"I really am," he said. "Although I must say, you've been a big help. Thank you for being beautiful and making it so easy."

"You're the only person who's ever called me beautiful," she said.

Impossible. "People tell you you're beautiful all the time. Rudy said it just this afternoon."

"They say it in a casual, flirty kind of way. You say it as if you really mean it."

"Because I do." So did everyone else who'd ever said it to her. It was adorable the way she didn't get it.

"Thank you."

She withdrew her foot from his grasp and rose to her knees next to him. She hesitated, but only for a second, before straddling his thighs. She wrapped her arms around his neck and leaned forward to kiss him.

There was a world of difference between kissing a woman and being kissed. Hannah started out so tentative and sweet that he thought his heart might explode through his chest. He couldn't claim an instant erection, however. That had already been making its presence known since before the movie even began.

He ran his hands up her thighs, his fingertips gliding over her soft, silky skin and under the skirt of her dress until they connected with the straps of a thong. She made soft, breathless sounds against his lips as he traced a finger along the crease of her buttocks. If he recalled correctly—and he did—then that thong should be paired with a demicup bra crafted of sheer lace and light satin. He loved all her unique pieces—the sweet and the sexy, the fragile innocence combined with the hot businesswoman who fixed her own truck.

"If we keep this up, the night is going to end with more than a kiss," he said, giving her fair warning. "Maybe we should have a talk about protection."

"I've been tested for every sexually transmitted disease my doctor could think of. The tests all came back negative," she said. "You're a doctor. I assume you know how to protect yourself."

"I do and I'm clean." The healthcare professional in him couldn't let her last comment pass, however. He'd used a condom the first time they'd had sex because they hadn't slowed down long enough to have this talk first. Now he knew he should have wondered why that might be, because her innocence in certain areas was showing. "But you shouldn't assume something like that. Doctors can be selfish bastards, too." The same as cheating ex-boyfriends. "Plus, protection involves more than STDs."

"I use birth control. To stay regular, Doctor," she said primly. "Not because I'm easy."

He fought back a smile that she thought it had to be said. Holding it in made his cheek muscles hurt. "I can't say the same. When it comes to you, I'm incredibly easy. I have three condoms in my pocket tonight. Now I also feel selfish and so unprofessional."

"Not selfish and unprofessional at all. I think it's considerate of you to make house calls. But what made you so sure three condoms would be enough?" she asked, eyebrows raised. "You don't have any heart problems, do you?"

"We haven't even begun, and already, I have performance anxiety."

"Don't worry, we can start off with something simple."

Simple.

He had no intentions of making love to her in a dull, conventional manner, if that was what she inferred—or of ever letting their love life become stale, either. She was a tactile, sensual woman, although even she might not know the full extent of it, yet. Their first night together, she'd been so curious. So eager. So willing to do whatever he asked. She was only inhibited in that she was used to traditional. He had a cure for that.

Last time, they'd had the possibility of someone walking in on them to contend with, which was why they'd remained partially clothed. Hannah had sat on his lap, just like this, with her dress hiked to her hips and the straps of her dress at her waist. She'd looked so beautiful, but they'd been flirting with each other all night, and riding a high—so to speak—so it had been glorious, but far too quick. He'd left her satisfied, though. Her orgasm hadn't been faked. The second one either, although he'd had to be more creative with that one. He'd start off with creativity, tonight.

"Them's fightin' words, ma'am. Challenge accepted."

He tipped her off his lap and onto the sofa, positioning her arms over her head. Then slowly, while she watched him, he began removing the pins from her hair, one at a time, untangling the soft strands and smoothing them out until her tresses were free. He enjoyed the feel of them as they slid over his hands and between his fingers.

"Normally, I'd suggest we help each other undress," he said. "We still can. I'm more than happy to remove your clothes for you. But it occurs to me that you've never seen me perform. Want to find out why I earned the big tips when I was stripping?"

"I already know. I saw you dance at the wedding."

"If you thought that was a stripper show, then you've never seen a real performance, before. I need music." He grabbed his phone and thumbed in Man 2 Man's "Male Stripper" off YouTube. He liked the quick Eurobeat because he could take off his clothes as fast or as slow as he wanted.

Tonight, he opted for slow. He got as far as his trousers by the end of the song.

From there, the show became a team effort. The thong disappeared. Then the dress. He discovered she wore the type of bra he particularly enjoyed. He dragged a finger along the tops of the cups before the bra joined the pile of clothes on the floor. She unfastened his pants and worked them down his thighs, then, while on her knees, freed his erection from his shorts. She took it in her hand and gave the tip an experimental lick with her tongue, then traced the rim, her eyes fastened on his. He felt the jolt all the way up his spine and down the backs of his legs.

He definitely was not going to make love to her in a traditional way.

"Come here," he said, and seconds later, had her bent over the back of the sofa so that she had her back to him, her buttocks resting against the fronts of his thighs, with his erection cradled between the rounds of her cheeks and his chest pressed to her shoulders. He smoothed her hair to the side and nuzzled her throat while he ran his hand over her hip to her firm belly. She had smooth, beautiful skin that soaked up the faint light in the room and he loved to touch every inch of her. She clutched the sofa with both hands and moaned when he stroked the underside of her breast and lightly tugged at the nipple.

"It's okay to talk during sex. You can tell me what you'd like me to do for you," he said. "My imagination's pretty good. I can come up with lots of things on my own. But let's start with what you think you might like."

"I want you inside me," she said.

And didn't those words, and the soft, eager tone in which they were uttered, make him so ready to comply. But he'd thought about her for months. Dreamed of her. *Wanted* her. And he wanted her to want him at least half as much, so tonight was about her, and learning what gave her the most pleasure.

"And I will be," he said, praying he wasn't overplaying his hand, and that he could last a little while longer, since he'd started this game. "But if I do that, then it's over too soon and there's so much more I can do for you, first. Use your imagination and ask me for anything. I promise, you won't shock me. What do you like?"

"I like when you touch me. Here." She guided his hand into the place between her thighs. He eased a finger inside her. She was so warm and ready—so freaking *hot* for him—that he almost reconsidered allowing their lovemaking session to draw out any longer.

He began stroking her cleft, in and out, and breathed into her ear. "Like this?"

"Yes." She arched her back, pressing tighter against him, and sighed with such pleasure, his testicles clenched in response. "*Yes.*"

So much for drawing things out. He slid inside her from behind, slowly, carefully, until she writhed beneath his touch and begged him for more. He held one hand against her belly, helping her steady herself as she clutched the back of the sofa, and palmed her hip with the other, fighting hard for control, but he was well past the point where he could deny his own urges. He thrust harder, and deeper, and oh, God, but she felt so magnificent around him as tiny, internal muscles gripped and massaged his hard length. He paused for a second, just to enjoy the sensations she gave him, then set the rhythm as she moved along with him to absorb every thrust. He smoothed his palm along the length of her arched spine and whispered encouragement as he felt her draw closer to orgasm.

"Let it go," he said, his knees shaking from the effort of

holding back.

Her whole body trembled. The gripping and massaging sensations washed over him in a tsunami of indescribable pleasure. When she cried out, Dallas, caught up in her release, lost control of his own. A harsh, guttural groan escaped him as he came. After that, for long moments, there was nothing but the sounds of them breathing.

Withdrawing, leaving all of that warmth and pleasure, nearly had him in tears. He gathered her into his arms for fear they both might collapse. A trip to the emergency room so wasn't going to happen tonight.

"To the bedroom," he said, and stooping down, flipped her over his shoulder in a fireman's carry that soon had her breathless with laughter. He clapped his hand on her bare backside, which was so temptingly close to his face, and gave it a possessive rub.

He had great plans for it shortly.

✳

Hannah

"I'VE GOT TO go."

Dallas, half-dressed, was a sight to wake up to. It was barely six thirty and Hannah blinked against the too bright, too early, morning light. A pink, disposable razor had taken care of chin stubble that had rubbed the inside of her thighs in a manner she'd never experienced before and left her a touch sore—but in an excellent way. He'd showered, and his damp hair was a mass of black curls. He jerked his trousers on, not bothering with underwear so he took extra care with the zipper, and bent over the bed to kiss her first on the forehead, then the lips, while he buttoned his shirt.

"Can I see you again tonight?" he asked.

"I'd like that."

Hazel eyes grinned down at her. "Stay away from Gal Gadot."

"Don't worry. If she shows up, I'll introduce her to Tom Hardy."

Before she could doze off for another hour of sleep she badly needed, her phone rang somewhere in the living room. It was just like Dallas to call her before he'd even left the parking lot. Her foot caught in the comforter as she tumbled headlong out of bed and she banged her knee on the dresser before she dashed out of the bedroom.

A frantic search uncovered the phone under the sofa on the fifth ring. She answered before voice mail could pick up, already smiling, prepared to come up with a clever response to whatever he said, but anything clever vanished the moment she heard the familiar male voice.

"Hey, Hans. I'm in Grand. Mind if I drop by?" Tim said.

Chapter Eleven

Hannah

HER AIRLOCKED CHEST refused to decompress. Yes, she minded. She minded a lot.

Somehow, she managed to speak. "Why are you here?"

"I want to talk to you."

The speed with which her shock turned to rage left her dizzy. Blood pounded against the top of her head and drummed at her ears. How did he even dare? Especially now, when she was so happy? "We have nothing left to say to each other."

"Please, Hannah."

The naked plea in his voice made her even more angry. It meant something had gone wrong and he needed her to help sort it out. Their long history together also meant she was about to give in, making her furious with herself for it, too. At what point in their relationship had she become the one who'd fixed all his problems? When had she turned into his mother?

Why had he never grown up?

Because he'd never had to. And she was at least partly to blame.

She didn't want him in her personal space, however. They'd shared everything since they'd become a couple in high school, but not anymore. The Grand Master Brewery was all hers. So were the memories associated with it. Those memories included Dallas.

"I'll meet you for coffee," she said. "There's a little place on the waterfront called the Wayside Café. How about ten o'clock?"

The Wayside was a cute little hipster café that Hannah had only visited once or twice but really enjoyed. It smelled delicious. She arrived early and bought a coffee and a freshly baked chocolate croissant from the gleaming display cabinet for herself.

The morning was overcast and chilly—fall was on its way—but even so, she chose a round, cast-iron, two-seater table on the outdoor patio that overlooked the Yellowstone River. She admired the view of the quiet waters drifting past while she waited. A few boats were out, but they stayed well away from the boardwalk. Birds cried on the wetlands nearby. Something splashed in the water.

She yawned. Dallas had kept her up most of the night—something that hadn't happened in… ever. He was fun, and yet, he managed to be responsible, too. She didn't know where their relationship was headed, but after months of upheaval she was finally in a good place, and she wasn't about to let Tim ruin it for her.

The door to the café opened. Tim appeared, coffee and muffin in hand, at exactly the same moment the sun burst through the clouds.

Of course it did. It always shone on him.

He looked much the same. Thinner, perhaps. Blond haired and blue eyed, he'd been the handsomest boy at Sweetheart High. She'd thought he was perfect. She'd crushed on him for months before he finally noticed her and asked her out. He'd played football back then and continued to carry the self-confidence that went with it to this day.

But the confidence Dallas displayed was far different from this. He cared about people. Tim, on the other hand, had already proven he cared about no one but himself. Why had it taken an affair for her to see it? When had he stopped seeming so perfect?

"Hannah."

Tim's voice caressed her in a way that had once made her feel so special. Not anymore. She glanced at her phone, checking for messages—nothing from Dallas—and barely acknowledged his greeting. "I've only got a few minutes," she said, before stowing the phone in her purse. "I'm scheduled to meet with one of my suppliers in half an hour."

"Thanks for seeing me." Cast-iron chair legs scraped the weathered wood of the deck as he sat down across from her. He blessed her with a smile dripping with fondness. "You look as beautiful as ever."

She couldn't remember the last time he'd told her she was beautiful. Dallas, on the other hand, said it often and always sounded as if he meant it, too. She could see it in his eyes when he looked at her, too. He made her feel as if the world revolved around her, as trite as that sounded.

"What did you want to talk to me about?" she asked, impatient for Tim to get to the point. What was so important that he had to drive all the way to Grand for it?

"I had to see you."

Hannah waited. He was uncomfortable with whatever he wanted to say. In the past, she would have helped him out. She saw no reason to make things easier for him now.

"What have you been up to? How is the brewery?" he asked. "From the looks of it, our business plan appears to be earning its A-plus."

Our business plan. Not *yours*.

A red haze clouded her vision. She blinked it away. She'd allow him to claim a share in the original idea, but the plan she'd ended up using was all hers and he couldn't take credit for that.

"I had to revise it significantly to make it fit a one-person operation, but I've managed to make it work," she said.

"I'm glad you decided to go ahead with it. I never doubted you'd make it a success." He broke off a chunk of muffin, tossed it into his mouth, then washed it down with a gulp of hot coffee. He played with the white ceramic mug for a moment. When he realized that she wasn't going to add anything more, he said, "My job was downsized."

"I'm sorry to hear that."

"It's for the best." He picked up her hand and held it even though she tried to pull it away. "I was hoping you'd give us—me—another chance. Grand could be a do-over for us. We could maybe think about starting that family we always dreamed of."

The rage she'd allowed to subside returned as a blazing inferno. They'd both claimed to want children. Now he tried to use them against her as a bargaining chip.

"What about…" She couldn't say it. She refused to admit knowing the woman's name. She'd creeped her on Facebook a few times more than was healthy, then loathed herself for it.

"Jennifer?" Tim avoided her eyes. He gazed out over the river where silvery eddies swirled around and under the patio. His Adam's apple bobbled. "Funny how you don't realize how much better you had it until it's too late."

Then, the whole story poured out. His new girlfriend left him when he lost his job.

Hannah had thought for months about what she might say or do if this moment should come, but found she couldn't be mean, no matter how much he deserved it. Once the flash of rage burned itself out, she felt nothing but…

Nothing. She'd already learned that getting even wasn't for her.

She pried her fingers free. "Honestly, you were right to

leave me." *Although you might have done it in a kinder, more respectful way.* "We were holding each other back. We both have different dreams now. You've hit a temporary snag, but you'll recover from it. Give it time." She should stop now. She wasn't his personal cheerleader, anymore.

"I don't want time. I want us to go back to the way things were. I want us to build the future together that we always planned on. Give me another chance. I promise I'll do better this time. I'll be the man you deserve. I love you, Hannah. I need you."

He didn't need her as much as he wanted her to make his decisions for him. And as for his declaration of love...

She wondered which of them had stopped loving the other first. Because she didn't love him. Not in the same way. He didn't make her heart stutter. He didn't steal her breath. He didn't make her long to hear his voice, or to watch him when he thought she wasn't looking. He didn't make her laugh. He didn't fill her with admiration and wonder that something so perfect could exist.

But this inability to think for himself and accept responsibility for his actions was partly her doing. They'd had plenty of problems over the years, meaning they'd both grown far too accustomed to a particular pattern of anger and forgiveness.

Except that pattern had never included other women before. He'd crossed a line, and now, the pattern had changed. He'd thrown away any chance for happiness they might have had. He didn't get to ruin things with Dallas for her, too.

"It's too late to go back to the way things were. Take some time to think about what you really want out of life, then work toward it. You don't need me for that. You don't need Jennifer, either," she added, even though he didn't deserve that small affirmation of his self-worth. His ego had always been healthy.

"I'm not giving up on us."

"There is no *us*, anymore." She stood. So did he. She picked up her purse. "I'm seeing someone."

He looked stricken. "I don't care who you've been sleeping with. I'll get past it."

Which pretty much meant he wouldn't, if that was the first place his head went. She didn't think she'd get past his affairs either, so in that regard, they were even.

"You gave up your rights to an opinion on my sleeping arrangements when you neglected to tell me about the changes you made to your own," she said coldly. "Go back to Bozeman. There are plenty of opportunities for someone with a business degree."

"There's a brewery right here that could use me and my degree to help run it."

A knot in her stomach awoke her to the reality of what he'd really come to Grand for, and while he might believe otherwise, ultimately, it wasn't for her. The brewery, either. She represented financial security to him. She'd paid for his education. Then, when he left, he took half of the money from their joint bank account too, even though her salary was direct deposited into it while his wasn't.

But he believed he was entitled to it and the state of Montana agreed. They'd presented themselves as married, which meant as far as the state was concerned, any assets were half his, so she'd written the money off as a hard lesson learned. They really had shared everything for far too long, however, if he believed he could walk back into her life and assume half of what was rightfully hers, as if nothing had happened, despite having left her for someone else.

"The brewery is mine, and I don't need help to run it. I'm doing just fine on my own," she said.

"I can see that." He thrust his hands in his jacket pockets, looking lost and forlorn. "Could you at least lend me some money until I find another job?"

She should say no. He'd gotten so much from her already. Instead, she asked, "How much do you need?"

"A thousand. For rent and to make car payments."

A *thousand.*

She was still angry with him over the affairs. He'd crushed her as if she meant nothing to him. Now, here he was, asking for money as if she were his personal banker. The selfish jerk. But she also felt guilty that he'd noticed something missing between them and she hadn't. She'd been too busy paying their bills and making plans for their future—plans that he'd been silent on, she now realized, so in some ways, she was as selfish as he was. She'd had a goal and she'd forced it on him.

That was why she said yes to the loan, even though she didn't have the money to spare. "I'll send you an e-transfer. You can pay me back when you can afford it." She turned away, knowing she'd likely never see it again.

"Hannah?"

She already had her hand on the café's glass patio door when he stopped her. "Yes?"

"Who is he?"

She wasn't giving him Dallas's name. Much like the brewery, he was a part of her life that Tim had no right to touch. "It doesn't matter."

"I suppose not." Tim hesitated, as if reconsidering what he'd intended to say, then plunged ahead with it, anyway. "I love you, Hans. I always have and I always will. And I know I don't deserve you anymore, but I don't want to see you get hurt. Again, I mean. I'm so sorry. It's just… Don't make the same mistake I did. Don't rush into a new relationship, okay?"

She couldn't allow that comment to pass. She had no reason to feel guilty about Dallas. Not now, and not for what happened at the wedding, either. "I'm not the one rushing into anything," she said. "You had an affair. *You.* Two of them, in fact—because yes, one-night stands do count. Obviously, you were looking for something different from what we had. Now, so am I."

She jerked the patio door open. Inside the café, she saw a

familiar face at the counter when she walked past it on her way to the main door off Yellowstone Drive. Ryan O'Connell. Dallas's friend. The Endeavour owner who'd ordered her beer for their open house. She'd only met him the once.

"Hi, Hannah," Ryan said as she squeezed between him and the cluster of café tables facing the counter. He carried three large coffees tucked in a biodegradable foam tray and a greasy brown bag.

"Hi." She flashed him an absentminded smile, but didn't slow down. Her head was already back on her business and the fresh batch of beer she'd begun—but it was mostly on Dallas, who she'd see that evening. She kicked herself for allowing Tim to get inside her head and manipulate her by planting doubts. She and Dallas were having fun together. Enjoying each other. They weren't rushing into anything. Not the way Tim had.

Were they?

✳

Dallas

"THANKS." DALLAS ACCEPTED the hot coffee and warm cinnamon bun Ryan offered.

The three friends had met up in the hospital's staff lounge for a quick coffee break together. They occupied a table at the far end of the room so they could carry on what passed for a private conversation in Grand, meaning the two young, giggling nurses seated next to the door pretended they weren't trying to listen in. Everyone learned that Dan had to work that evening, while Ryan planned to take the ranch's new Bell LongRanger helicopter out to help some of the hired hands round up and move beef cattle to fresh grazing ground closer to the main ranch. They could expect snow in another month and pastures would need to be fenced.

All of which left Dallas free to spend tonight with Hannah, too. In his head, he began making plans. He'd be on call, but unless the county's idiot sheriff got himself shot again, that usually meant nothing more than a few phone consultations. He'd run home for a change of clothes, then grab focaccia and roasted vegetable sandwiches from the Wayside for their dinner, and he'd help Hannah wait tables until closing. His shift changed tomorrow—twelve noon to midnight—so in the morning, they could sleep in. Next week, he and the guys were off on their "corporate retreat" and he wanted to spend as much time with her as he could before then.

"And then I said Dallas would be perfect for the bull riding exhibition. Danger is his middle name," Ryan was saying.

"What are we talking about?" Dallas asked, abruptly dragged back to the conversation when he heard his name.

By the sounds of it, nothing good.

"I'd forgotten how focused he can get when there's a woman in his life," Dan said to Ryan, one blond eyebrow drawn aloft to express his amusement. "It's been so long."

He'd zoned out for a moment. It wasn't as if Dan didn't have the same problem after an evening with Jazz. "What did I miss?"

"Ryan wants us to organize and operate a rodeo," Dan said.

Ryan's fascination with rodeos was legend. He'd worked as an operations manager for an auction and rodeo house in Texas after college. It was the longest he'd stuck with a career choice. "Not just any rodeo," he clarified. "I want Grand to host a PRCA-sanctioned event. I want us to position ourselves to take over as host of the Montana Circuit Finals in a few years." The PRCA was the Professional Rodeo Cowboys Association. The Montana Circuit Finals were held in January each year, which meant the Endeavour would have to build an indoor arena.

Dallas tallied up the ranch's current investments in his head. They funded smoke jumping services for the state of Montana and a general aviation airport for Custer County. They were in the process of building a free clinic for the town and surrounding areas, which should be operational by the new year. Ryan was taking on a group home for at-risk youth as soon as he could get the paperwork in order. They'd built bunkhouses for the kids already, as well as new bunkhouses for the local hired hands. They'd invested in Tennessee Walkers, which was no moneymaker either. Now they were talking about adding a rodeo to the mix. That was a lot of cash to lay out—not to mention the hours they'd be required to expend.

As much work as the Endeavour's ventures might make for Dallas and Dan, however, for Ryan, it was about twenty times more. Dallas and Dan often felt more like permanent residents at a high-end dude ranch. The annual cattle roundup was scheduled to happen mid-October and they'd already booked vacation time off so they could ride along, mostly for fun. Ryan, on the other hand, treated the roundup as if his next meal depended on it.

He managed all of their finances. He oversaw the ranch's daily operations, although they did have managers to help him. Now he wanted to take on a rodeo, too. And not just any rodeo—he wanted it to be on the circuit, with an eye on the finals. That was a serious investment of time and money. Dallas wasn't sure what to say.

Dan, always the voice of reason, didn't have the same problem. "I say we put it to a vote. Everyone who thinks Ryan should be allowed to have his rodeo, but only if he hires the right people to manage and promote it, and lets them do their jobs without any micromanagement on his part, raise your right hand." Dallas and Dan's hands shot up. "Two out of three. Motion carried."

"That didn't go the way I expected," Ryan said.

"That's because Dallie and I aren't crazy," Dan replied. His rubber-tipped chair legs squealed against the tile floor as he stood and picked up his empty cup. "I've got to get back to work. See you guys later."

The two nurses had also finished their coffee by now and couldn't seem to find any other good reason to linger. They rinsed their cups at the sink and stowed them in the dishwasher, then waved at Dallas on their way out behind Dan. Dallas waved back, tossing in a friendly grin for good measure. He liked the nurses here, and they seemed to like him, although he suspected their friendliness had more to do with upcoming positions at the free clinic than his sparkling wit. Regular clinic hours were a lot better than hospital shiftwork.

"I have no idea how someone so smart can be such a dumbass," Ryan said.

It took Dallas a second to figure out Ryan meant him. "What are you talking about now?" he asked, feeling like they'd had this conversation already. "What have I done?"

Ryan, the buzzkill, stroked his chin with his fingers and studied him through eyes brimming with pity. "I don't understand why I keep having to explain this to you. There are several billion reasons why you can't be that friendly with the single nurses on staff."

"I work with them. I was just being polite," Dallas protested.

"No offense, but you don't always read women right."

He was about to argue the point, then remembered Simone. "No one is ever right one hundred percent of the time."

"I'm not sure you even hit fifty percent."

"I only have to read Hannah, and so far, I'm doing okay." Last night was a good indicator of that.

He must have looked a little too smug about it though, because Ryan frowned. "About that… I bumped into Hannah at the Wayside," he said.

"So?" Dallas dangled his half-finished cup by the rim to illustrate the fact. "Along with most of the town. They make the best coffee. I hear it's a great way to start the morning off right."

"She wasn't alone."

A tiny bit of his good mood seeped away. He'd left her in bed, planning her day. She hadn't said a thing to him about meeting up with anyone. He plunked his cup down. Normally, he respected Ryan's deep-seated need to protect the people closest to him. He had trust issues that years of therapy hadn't managed to cure. "She's allowed to hang out with whoever she wants." Even if she'd said nothing to him about it.

"Sorry, Dallas. It's just that their conversation looked kind of intense. At one point he was holding her hand. *He* was holding *hers*," Ryan repeated hastily, apparently not having the same problem with reading people as he claimed Dallas did. "All I'm trying to say is that you have to be more careful about the people you let get close to you. Are you sure the old boyfriend is really out of the picture?"

"Positive." Hannah would have told him if her ex-boyfriend was in town. Unless, of course, she hadn't found out about it until after he'd left for work. She wouldn't have met him for coffee, though. No way.

"Forget I said anything," Ryan said. "You know how paranoid I can be."

Too late. Dallas's good mood had been flushed down the toilet and was currently swirling the drain. Ryan hadn't made any mistake and they both knew it. Whoever she'd met with, she knew him well.

But Dallas wasn't going to jump to any conclusions. Whatever reason Hannah had for meeting someone at the Wayside, it had definitely come up at the last minute. The man could have been anyone, too. It could have been one of her brothers. Her brother Blaise definitely fit the intense description. And it would be just like him to drop in on her unannounced.

She'd likely tell him all about it when he saw her that evening.

Chapter Twelve

Hannah

HANNAH INTENDED TO tell Dallas she'd had coffee with Tim as soon as she figured out how to best bring it up. While she didn't want to pretend it didn't matter, she also didn't want it to seem too important. She wanted to get the mix right so it didn't lead to an argument it didn't warrant.

And yet, as Dallas dropped his overnight bag by the door, and set the dinner he'd brought on the kitchen island, she had to wonder if their relationship might be progressing a little too quickly, at that. Her expectations of him seemed impossibly high. There didn't appear to be anything he couldn't handle. Nobody was perfect. When would she start to notice his faults?

He didn't give her a chance to dwell on her doubts. He scooped her into his arms and kissed her until she was breathless and clinging to him for support.

"You're so much nicer to come home to at the end of a really long day than Ryan and Dan," he said, smiling at her with amber-flecked eyes bright as stars. "They complain when I kiss them like that."

She buried her face in the front of his shirt. He smelled of hospital, her almond shampoo, and freshly pressed cotton. The crisp fabric crinkled under her fingers as she ran her palms over his chest. "Maybe they heard you were cheating on them with Tom Hardy."

"Tom and I are finished. I don't need him, now that I have you."

Too fast, her head whispered. Her heart couldn't hold all the things he made it feel.

"What made the day longer than normal?" she asked, turning the conversation back to him.

"I couldn't wait to see you again."

"That's so sweet." She threaded her arms around his neck. "What was the real reason?"

Because there was one. She felt it. The usual smile in his eyes hid something deeper and darker behind it tonight. It relieved her a little. It made him seem more human.

He disentangled himself. "It doesn't matter. It's over and done with. We should eat while the sandwiches are still warm."

She didn't care how quickly things were moving between them right now. If something at work affected him enough to put that dark look in his eyes, she wanted to know all about it in case she could help. He didn't get to pull away from her whenever he had a bad day. "If it matters to you, it matters to me. Let's talk it out."

He studied her for a moment. "A man lost his hand in a farm accident, today."

She caught her breath. "The poor man. I'm so sorry."

"Me too. There wasn't anything I could do for him other than keep him stable until the trauma surgeon arrived. But I'm okay, Hannah. It's not about me. He's got the longer haul ahead of him. It's hard to see a young guy have his whole life derailed because he chose to try and unclog a grain auger with his bare hands, that's all. He's lucky he didn't lose both. Or his life." The darkness was already receding as the humor returned. "I admit I'll be glad when the free clinic is ready and I can move back into family medicine, although to be honest, vaccinating babies isn't as much fun as you'd think, either. Every job has its downside."

And he used humor to balance his out.

"Remind me never to bring my children to you for their shots," she said, playing along.

"No worries there. Doctors aren't supposed to treat family members anyway."

He was only kidding around. The comment meant nothing. There was no need for her to feel this strange combination of terror and longing, as if she'd glimpsed something she desperately wanted but hadn't yet figured out the catch. There was always a catch.

"Did I say something wrong?" Dallas asked, picking up on her mood.

"No. I was thinking I couldn't do what you do. I can't imagine the level of stress you have to deal with."

"The trick is to find a good stress reliever. And I know just the thing." He took a step toward her, his meaning clear.

Her mood instantly lightened, feeding off his, her concerns slipping away. She backed up, spun, and put the island between them. "Forget it. The taproom opens in…" She glanced at the microwave clock. "Forty-five minutes."

He shrugged. "Plenty of time. We might have to dispense with the foreplay, though."

She feigned outrage. "No way. That's the best part."

He ducked left, so she dodged to the right. They circled the island.

"Okay. Let's sort this out," he said. "Compromise. I'll give you five minutes of foreplay if you give me ten minutes of oral sex. You usually take about two minutes to reach an orgasm after penetration. I should be warmed up enough by then to perform, but I'll spot you three more minutes just in case. That's twenty minutes, which leaves twenty-five minutes to eat dinner."

"None of that sounds remotely fair. Or even accurate," Hannah said, laughing too hard by now to check his math or even seriously object. "Counter offer. Fifteen minutes of foreplay—which might or might not include oral sex, but if it does, we take turns fifty-fifty—ten minutes of the actual act, then another ten minutes of post-coital cuddling. That leaves…" She took a wild guess. "Twenty minutes for food."

"Holy crap. What does this say about our public school system? And who does your bookkeeping? Because with math skills like that, it can't possibly be you," Dallas said, his hand over his heart as if to contain his shock. "And ten minutes for cuddling? What am I, a machine?"

He planted both hands on the counter and looked like he fully intended to vault it. Hannah wouldn't put it past him, so she broke and ran for the bedroom. He caught her before she could get the door closed, scooped her up by the waist, and tossed her, shrieking with laughter, onto the bed. He landed beside her, all six-plus, sexy feet of him.

He smoothed her hair off her face with a lazy finger. "We could always get the cuddling out of the way now and save the best part for later," he suggested, his voice warm and husky and making her head swirl with endless possibilities.

She could fall in love with him so easily—meaning things really were happening too fast. Less than a year ago, she'd been living with a man she'd loved for more than half her life.

She almost told Dallas about having coffee with Tim at the Wayside right then, but he'd already had a rough day and didn't need her adding to it. A man losing a hand trumped foolish doubts raised by an ex-boyfriend who had no claim to her anymore.

She suddenly wanted Dallas. Badly. To prove she was his.

She began unbuttoning his shirt. "Ten minutes of sex.

Straight up. We'll bank the foreplay and the cuddling for some night we're both too tired to perform."

"Deal," Dallas said.

He ducked a palm under her T-shirt to rest on her belly. His lips and his fingers trickled heat along her flushed skin. Within minutes, they were both undressed and wrapped up in each other. He moved gently at first, then, at her insistence, with greater abandon. She arched her back as her orgasm began, lost to all but the waves of pleasure he gave her, and grasped his hips until she heard his harsh breaths and felt him stiffen, too.

Long moments later, she came back to her surroundings. He rolled to the side, taking her with him, so that she lay on top staring down at him with him still inside her. He threw an arm over his eyes and groaned.

"I hope you weren't timing that," he said, peering at her from under his elbow, "because if so, I think I just disgraced myself and most of mankind."

She brushed a kiss along the rough edge of his jaw that prickled her lips and waited for her erratic heart rate to sort itself out. "I can't speak for mankind, but as far as this woman's concerned, I have no complaints."

✳

THEY MADE IT downstairs to the taproom with five minutes to spare. Dallas unlocked the door while she opened the cash.

Monday nights were slow. She only had two customers—cowboys who worked on the Endeavour Ranch. Dallas stopped to talk to them and buy them each a beer before pulling a table up to the bar.

"How about a game of chess to kill time?" he suggested to Hannah.

"I'm terrible at it," she warned him, then proceeded to win the first game in less than ten moves.

"Huh." Dallas tipped his king. "I've been fleeced."

"Did you really think I'd have a games theme for my business and not be any good at them?" she asked.

"Pretty girls aren't supposed to be smart."

"You just added ten minutes to cuddling, wise guy. I—" The outer door opened before she could finish her sentence. She glanced over to see who it could be. She'd half hoped to be able to close up early so she and Dallas could pick up where they'd left off at the start of the evening. It was almost ten o'clock and the two cowboys looked ready to call it a night.

A panicky sensation slithered over her skin when she saw the tall, athletic man with the casually ruffled blond hair, dressed to impress in a smart business suit. What was Tim doing here?

His gaze swept the room, found her, then shifted to Dallas, where it lingered too long. Hannah upset one of the chess pieces in her haste to intercept him before he could approach their table. She wasn't about to introduce the two men.

She rushed over to cut him off before he'd made it half-way across the room. "What are you doing here?" she asked.

He smiled at her as if there were no one else in the room. That smile bruised her heart. It took her back to the days when they'd first moved in together. They'd been eighteen, straight out of high school, and she'd been so in love. Whatever happened between them? What had gone wrong?

Why hadn't she been enough?

"I wanted to see the Grand Master Brewery for myself. Love the name, by the way," he said.

"Go away," Hannah said quietly. "Leave me alone."

"I can't do that," Tim said, keeping his voice down too, shrinking the room to the two of them. "I love you, Hans. I need to know you're okay and aren't making a mistake just because you're angry with me. I screwed up, yes. I own it. But I found a place in Grand to stay and I have a job interview next week." He gazed past her toward where Dallas was setting up the chessboard for a rematch. "So that's my competition."

He shouldered past her and strode over to Dallas. Hannah had no way to stop him. She trailed behind him, kicking herself for giving him the money to stay. If she hadn't, he'd have likely gone to his parents in Sweetheart for help.

"Hi," he said to Dallas, extending a hand. "Tim Ryder. You are…"

Dallas glanced at the hand offered to him but kept his own on the table. He toyed with the white bishop. He met Tim's eyes. "A friend of Hannah's."

Tim slowly withdrew his hand. His attitude clearly said, *So this is how it's going to be.* Hannah's heart sank. He liked a challenge. He pulled up a chair and sat down. "A good friend, I take it."

"I like to think so, but you can take it however you want."

The two cowboys had figured out that something far more interesting was going down and abandoned their board game. They sipped at their beers as they sat back to watch.

"You're being an ass," Hannah said to Tim. It was too late to worry about him making a scene. Her new fear was that the Endeavour cowboys might feel obligated to step in on Dallas's behalf. For now, they appeared content to wait and see how things would unfold.

"I'd like a beer. You can bring one for your friend, too," Tim said to her. "It's on me."

Hannah looked at Dallas, uncertain as to what she should do and hoping for guidance. The two men were so completely different. On the surface, Tim gave the more polished impression. If a stranger were asked to choose which of the two was more successful, they'd pick him based on first impressions alone. Dallas, on the other hand, looked more like a tousled, decadent god who'd just rolled out of some Greek maiden's bed. She might have had something to do with that image.

"I'll take a blond," Dallas said to her, his eyes calm and expression unreadable.

She wished that she'd told him she'd had coffee with Tim. She should have given him more credit. Instead, she felt as if she'd been caught in a lie. Which, in fact, she had. It was an old habit. She'd often held things back when she didn't have the mental energy to get into an argument with Tim. He liked to fight whereas she usually—but not always—gave in.

"Surprise me," Tim said. "You know what I like." He adjusted the cuffs of his shirt as he examined the board. "How about a game of chess while we drink?" he suggested to Dallas.

"No," Hannah interrupted. "You can't have a beer and you aren't playing chess. I want you to leave."

For a long moment, she thought he might argue with her. She had no idea how Dallas might react if he did. This moment really drove home that she didn't know Dallas very well yet. The silence stretched until it settled over the entire room. The two cowboys looked ready to intercede. They watched Dallas closely, taking their cues from him.

"Okay," Tim finally said, clearly not liking the odds—or the situation. This had to be a new experience for him. He'd been popular in high school and college. He truly enjoyed meeting new people. Marketing had been the perfect career path for him. She'd always felt so lucky that of all the girls he could have had, he'd chosen her. She began to feel sorry for him. Just a little. But then, he threw her under the bus. "How about we meet up for coffee again tomorrow morning?" he suggested, his smile just for her. "You have my number. Call me."

The cowboys packed up their game and signaled good night on their way out the door behind him. She dropped into his vacated chair.

Dallas didn't say anything. He simply sat across the table from her and waited while she got the chaos in her head straightened out.

"He called me this morning right after you left. I didn't check the number," she blurted out in a rush. "I thought it was you or I wouldn't have answered the phone. He said he wanted to talk. I knew he wouldn't give up, and I didn't want him to come here, so I suggested I meet him for coffee. He told me he lost his job and his new girlfriend left him. He asked if he could borrow enough money to make his car payment and rent, and to hold him over until he can find something new. I didn't know he'd use the money to find an apartment in Grand. He has a job interview here next week, too."

He twirled the bishop, making it dance. "How do you feel about all of this?"

"Like I'm being dragged by my heels, kicking and screaming, back to my life the way it was a year ago, except now it's all twisted and bent and broken," she confessed. "I don't want that life anymore," she hurried on. "I would have told you about coffee"—at least, she hoped she would have—"except you'd already had a bad day and I didn't want to add to it."

"How much money did you lend him?"

"A thousand dollars." She had no reason to feel defensive about it, either. It was her money. She could do whatever she liked with it.

"Is this something I should be worried about?" Dallas asked.

"Absolutely not."

He continued twirling the bishop. Then, he set it carefully upright on its home square. "Do you want me to stay tonight or would you rather I go home?"

She wanted him to stay. She wanted him to chase her around the apartment and tell her how beautiful she was. She wanted the cuddling and foreplay he owed her. But there was no way she could ask for any of that tonight. Not while she had the past in her head. She and Tim had to settle a few things.

"Would you mind going home?" she asked around the lump in her throat, because she also wanted some space. She'd handled everything so badly and she wouldn't be able to think it all through if Dallas were with her.

"No." He leaned across the table, cupped her face in his hands, and kissed her. "But I will mind if you have coffee with him again," he added.

Chapter Thirteen

Dallas

"LOOK," RYAN SHOUTED over the beat of the helicopter blades. He pointed. Below them, a herd of a hundred or more elk coiled around the base of Evenstone Mountain.

At four thousand feet, Evenstone wasn't one of the more impressive land masses in Montana, and it didn't form part of the Rockies, but it did offer a spectacular view of the surrounding terrain and provided shelter to an abundance of local wildlife.

Ryan circled a few times before bringing the helicopter down in a clearing surrounded by scraggly ponderosas, a smattering of limber pine, and a blade-propelled profusion of airborne debris. They planned to camp on top of one of the sandstone buttes overlooking the Tongue River, but it meant they'd have to hike because this was as close as Ryan could get to the buttes and guarantee a safe landing.

They left their fishing gear stowed in the helicopter to be retrieved in a couple of days. This section of the Badlands was private property, owned by the Endeavour, and virtually inaccessible except by air, so the potential for damage or theft was slim to none. Anyone determined enough could likely reach the clearing by ATV, but that possibility was even more remote than the area itself.

They donned backpacks and began the upward trek. A faint trail carved by erosion and surefooted elk circled the butte. Rumor had it that mountain goats once roamed Evenstone too, but no signs of them had been seen in years. Dallas suspected they'd been hunted out.

It took them several hours to reach the top of Buffalo Butte. Dan's leg wound wasn't one hundred percent yet and Dallas had to keep an eye on him to make sure he didn't overextend himself.

Finally, however, Dallas stood at the edge of the butte and breathed deep. The sharp tang of pine drifting skyward from the sparse copse below bit the inside of his nose. The Tongue River formed a thin ribbon of silver that trickled past the base of the butte. They'd left home just past six a.m. on a Saturday morning, and according to Dallas's stomach, it was now nearly lunchtime. They were going to eat, set up camp, and then he and Ryan were going to do some rock climbing while Dan read a book.

A few days away from the hospital would do him good. A few days away from Hannah would be good for them both. He'd been working late every night so he hadn't seen her since Monday, although they'd texted back and forth quite a bit. She knew he'd planned to make this week-long trip with his friends, that it was partly business, and he'd promised to call her as soon as he got back. They hadn't discussed Tim Ryder yet, but that moment was coming.

Would you mind going home?

He'd minded, all right. But what could he say? He'd once asked her if she'd ever take the guy back and she hadn't answered—which was exactly why he shouldn't have rushed her. She'd tried to tell him that she hadn't sorted out her feelings yet and he hadn't gotten the message. Hannah needed closure. He couldn't help her with that. If anything, he got in her way.

He had some things to sort out with her too, however. She seemed under the impression that sex was the only form of cheating there was. It was definitely a betrayal. A very intimate one. He wouldn't argue with that. But there was emotional cheating too, and she was coming very close to crossing a line that he couldn't ignore. He got that she felt loyalty to someone she'd been with for so long. She couldn't shut off her feelings, and he didn't expect that she should, but he didn't intend to draw up second behind someone who'd already forfeited the race.

He wasn't happy that Tim Ryder was in town with her and he wasn't—or that she might have a greater sense of loyalty to a man she'd been with for a very long time than she did to him. He didn't like that they'd had sex right after she'd had coffee with her ex, either. Being the punctuation mark on the end of her prior relationship—for a second time—didn't sit well. Not at all.

By the time he and Ryan returned from an afternoon of rock climbing, Dan had dinner already cooked. They ate, then after they'd cleaned up, settled in for a night of stargazing and a business discussion regarding their plans for the Endeavour's future.

Dallas was stretched out on his back on his sleeping bag between Ryan and Dan, his hands locked behind his head. There was nothing in the world quite like a Montana sky on a clear night. Stars salted the deep, midnight-blue backdrop. The Milky Way shot across the heavens in a swirling white tunnel. A massive moon had barely begun its slow crawl between the horizons.

A series of loud yips, howls, and barks cut through the air. Somewhere in the night coyotes hunted, most likely the elk they'd seen from the helicopter that morning. While they'd be hard-pressed to take on an elk already full grown, in a herd that size, there'd be the sick, the young, and the weak to take advantage of.

"You're awfully quiet tonight, Dallie," Dan said to him. "That's so unlike you."

"Just thinking. Have you ever noticed that the Milky Way looks very similar to what an Einstein-Rosen bridge must look like?" Dallas asked. "There's supposed to be a supermassive black hole at the Milky Way's heart but the gravitational pull suggests it's a wormhole."

Dan turned his head to the side so that he faced him.

"Thinking about Hannah, huh?" he said, proving it was hard to hide things from friends.

"Maybe."

Ryan spoke up from the darkness. "The guy she met for coffee turned out to be her ex, didn't he?"

"He's got a job interview in Grand and intends to stay. Not to mention she lent him money. He showed up at the taproom the other night while I was there, too." And then Hannah asked him for space. He left that part out.

"Ouch. What did you think of him?" Dan asked, zeroing in on what was important.

"Honestly?" Dallas said. "He seemed pretty sure of himself."

That was what stung the most. There was no denying Ryder knew Hannah well enough to play her and get under her skin. He'd likely needed the money he borrowed from her, but his real reason for asking for it would be because it gave him an excuse to keep reaching out. He'd repay her fifty dollars here, a hundred there, always in cash, and he'd make sure to bring it to her in person. When that was paid up, he'd borrow more. Thank God they hadn't had kids together or she'd never be rid of him.

"Things aren't always how they appear," Dan reminded him sympathetically. "Unless that rumor going around about you and Simone getting friendly in the garage during the open house happened exactly as eyewitness accounts appear to suggest."

He couldn't argue with that. "It didn't. Not exactly, no."

"If you don't want him in Grand, I can take care of that for you," Ryan offered.

"No!" Dan and Dallas both said at the same time, although Dan maybe more emphatically. Ryan's line between right and wrong got blurry, sometimes.

"She can handle him herself," Dallas felt obligated to add, because he believed it. It didn't mean he had to like it, however. "It's complicated, that's all. She was with him a long time."

"There are five stages of grief and loss—or seven, depending on who your therapist subscribes to—and they apply to all loss, including broken relationships," Ryan said, who'd had plenty of therapy and should be an expert, but really, he wasn't. He liked to parrot it back, but Dallas suspected none of it truly sank in. "Her ex showing up has caused a setback in the process for her. If she's loaned him money, then she's likely got some guilt happening. Over what, I can't say. Maybe you. Maybe she burned all of his belongings when they split up. Who knows? None of which means she wants him back. She'll likely get angry again any day now, and when she does, I wouldn't want to be either one of you—because you're both potential targets."

"Have you always been this much of a downer?" Dallas asked. "And if so, why am I just noticing it now?"

"Ignore Dr. Phil. Don't you know better than to take relationship advice from a guy who picks up his women outside of the men's room at rodeos? He's aggravated by all of the paperwork involved in setting up a group home and is taking it out on us," Dan said.

Ryan sighed. "It's true. The hoops never end. A case manager has to be assigned, and all of the plans for treatment programs reviewed. The high school has to approve the education plans. I have to hire staff. Not to mention, I need a board of directors. You two have both volunteered to be on it, by the way. And all before the Endeavour can open its doors."

"Jazz has the smoke jumper base under control so my obligations for that are met, and I have connections through the sheriff's department who can help me find the right people to work with at-risk youth on a ranch, so why not let me hire the staff for you?" Dan suggested.

"How are things going with Jazz, anyway?" Dallas asked, happy to have the subject shift off him. "Isn't she headed back to Helena soon?" The base was only open part of the year, at least for now, and Dan and Jazz were about to embark on a long-distance relationship because they both had other commitments.

"Things are great. It's going to be a long year of back-and-forth travel, but she's worth it," Dan said, with so much contentment that Dallas was almost sorry he asked. He'd had that same level of contentment within reach and then it slipped through his fingers. "Don't listen to Ryan. If she's the right woman, things will work out with Hannah, too."

"And if they don't, never fear. You've always got us to help keep you warm," Ryan said, and Dallas threw a pillow at him.

✳

Hannah

"WHAT'S THE MATTER?" Marsh asked.

They were watching a movie on the TV in his room because he hadn't felt up to the trip to the residents' lounge. Normally, Hannah would have tried to convince him to get out and socialize, but today, his color was poor and he seemed rather listless, so the nurses had propped him up with pillows in the armchair next to the window and she sat beside him. Rain spit at the glass. He'd lacked his usual enthusiasm when she walked in to visit, and hadn't been particularly engaged in the movie, so it surprised her that he noticed she wasn't herself.

"Nothing," she said.

A spark of interest animated his worn features. "Uh-oh. When a woman says nothing, it usually means a man ought to run. I'm afraid that's beyond me these days, so you might as well tell me what's put that gloom on your face."

"You don't want to hear about it," she said.

She'd grown to love Marsh, but she had doubts about spilling her relationship troubles to someone so old school.

He might not approve of her having lived with Tim. She definitely didn't plan to tell him how she'd first gotten involved with Dallas. Revenge sex was never something she'd be proud of.

"Problems with Dr. Dallie, I take it? Your date didn't go well?"

She didn't really have any problems with Dallas. If he weren't so wonderful, she wouldn't feel so much to blame. "The problem is me."

"There's another man," Marsh said, nodding. "Pretty girl like you likely has to beat them off with a stick."

Hannah laughed. He sounded so all-knowing and wise.

"What?" he demanded, showing more life. "I'm old. I'm not dead. Not yet, at least. I've learned a few things over the years."

She let the dead comment pass. "Promise you won't think less of me if I tell you."

A twinkle entered his eye. "If I have to promise, this should be good."

"Remember, you asked," she warned him. She left out the more intimate details, but told him everything else—about Tim, the affair, and how she'd moved to Grand to start a new life.

"So. Your ex-partner is in town and he's had a run of bad luck," Marsh said when she finished. "A man who cheats on a good woman is bound to realize his mistake sooner rather than later. Why is this a problem for you?"

"Because I don't want him here. I moved to Grand to get away from him."

"Why did you do that?" Marsh persisted. "Did you do something wrong, too?"

"No, I didn't," she said slowly. She'd been telling herself she hadn't, and her head knew she hadn't, but now, her heart finally began to believe it, too.

"Then why is his being here a problem for you? Do you still love him?"

"No." But that right there was the problem. Her head didn't love him. Her heart wasn't yet as fully convinced.

Marsh wasn't, either. "I'm not sure I believe you."

Hannah's eyes stung. "I can't seem to turn off my feelings for him the way he turned off his for me. I loved him for fifteen years. Then he turned into someone I don't know. Maybe I should have seen the changes, but I didn't. Whatever went wrong, I'm at least partly to blame."

Marsh gave some thought to her words before carefully picking his own to reply. "He likely never stopped loving you. It appears to me as if he's the type of man who gets restless, is all. Some women don't mind that. You do." He patted her hand. "He's not for you, darlin'. That doesn't mean you have to turn off your feelings. I'm sure you had plenty of good times together, despite how things ended. You got used to having him around. Like a favorite old pair of boots. But understand that if you do go back to him, the relationship ain't ever going to be equal. He sounds like a taker. You'd always be giving more."

"I won't go back to him," Hannah said. Her head wasn't stupid. Her heart was the dumb one. It couldn't seem to let go.

"Then what's the problem?"

"I'm sad and I'm angry that we lost what we might have had. He threw it away. I don't want to have any feelings for him anymore. I want to give them all to... someone else."

"I'm so old, sometimes I forget how tragic it is to be young." Humor smoothed the lines on Marsh's cheeks and crinkled his eyes. "No one's ever going to get one hundred percent of your feelings, Hannah. That's why God gifted you plenty enough to spread around."

It didn't feel like much of a gift. Mostly, her feelings swirled around inside her like twigs in an eddy, catching and snarling on every rock that they bumped into until they were all tangled together in one giant clump. "That's easy for you to say. You were married to the same woman for seventy-three years."

"Sure was. But she wasn't always married to me. Her first husband passed away after less than a year and she didn't think she'd ever love anyone again. I had to work hard to get her to notice me, let alone agree to marry me. And I never once asked her to turn off her feelings for him. We had a different relationship between us, that's all."

"How did you get through it?"

"It was harder for her. She went through the anger and

guilt, all the things you likely feel, except for different reasons. She'd lost someone important, which made her angry, and he'd never get a crack at a second chance the way she did, and that made her feel guilty and angry. All I did was hold her hand while she muddled it out. In the end she made room for me, too."

Hannah smoothed the rumpled cotton blanket over his knee, more to settle her thoughts than because the blanket needed straightening. Outside the window, the rain had quit throwing its temper tantrum and the sun beamed with relief. A lot of the weight she'd been feeling—weight she couldn't explain—shifted so it didn't seem as much of a burden.

"Why wouldn't she make room? You're pretty easy to love," she said.

Marsh grinned. "So is Dr. Dallie."

"He is," she confessed.

And she wished with all her heart that she'd loved him first. Then it wouldn't be in this mess.

Chapter Fourteen

Hannah

S HE COAXED HER truck into gear, and after giving it a quick pep talk, it staggered its way onto the street. The sky's gray, low-hanging belly suggested another downpour was pending. The nip in the air warned it might bring sleet with it, too.

While she was glad for the space Dallas gave her, she wished he hadn't given her quite so much. She longed to see him and begin making amends, but he and his friends would be gone the whole upcoming week. She had no way to reach him, either. The men had headed into the Badlands, where cell phone reception was either nonexistent or so sketchy as to be next to useless, for some rock climbing and fly-fishing. She hoped they'd prepared for the weather, because tonight promised to be wild.

Her check-engine light began to flash as she turned onto her street. Her heart sank. This was beyond her level of mechanical skill. She'd have to replace either the engine or the truck and she'd given away every spare penny she had.

Her brother would have told her to pull over and shut it down, but she didn't have much farther to go and it was already a dead man walking, so she kept on going.

Moments later, the truck limped into the parking lot behind the brewery, then coughed its last breath as she turned off the engine. A few spatters of rain hissed on the hood.

Poopy-sticks.

This was no big deal, she told herself. The truck had rolled off the lot during the Clinton administration. She'd known it wouldn't last forever. The warning signs it was on its last legs had definitely been there. She'd simply have to suspend her customer taxi service and hire a truck to make the few local product deliveries commitments she had. She'd get by.

Her phone jangled in her purse. It was the duty nurse at the home. "Hi Hannah," he said, "Marsh passed away in his sleep a few moments ago. He didn't have any immediate family, but I thought you might like to know." They'd found him when they took him a tray for dinner.

"Thank you," Hannah managed to say, although her insides were numb. If she'd stayed another half hour, he wouldn't have died alone. She stared at the phone in her hand. She tried Dallas's number without any real hope, but the call didn't go through, so she sent him a text. *Call me when you get a chance pls.*

Someone knocked on her window, making her jump.

Tim. One more thing she didn't need. She'd been so

caught up in the shock over Marsh that she hadn't paid any attention to the other cars in the lot. Neighbors often parked here on street cleaning nights. She dropped her phone in her purse, blinked the tears back, got her *fight or flight* instincts under control, and rolled down her window.

Tim's expression grew concerned when he noticed the look in her face.

"Hey, Hans. You okay?"

It was on the tip of her tongue to tell him about Marsh. She'd told him everything for years. He knew all of her secrets—or most of them, at least—but she couldn't bring herself to say anything because Tim hadn't known Marsh. He didn't know how special he was. He'd hear that Marsh was ninety-eight, and say he'd lived a full life, which was true enough, but it was Marsh's contributions to her life, not hers to his, that she would miss. Her throat went dry and sticky. The backs of her eyes burned. She missed Dallas so much.

"My truck died," she said.

"And you gave me the last of your money, didn't you?" Tim rubbed the back of his neck, true remorse on his face. "I'll get it back to you as soon as I can, Hans. I promise. You can borrow my car, if you like. I don't mind walking."

The gesture was second nature, the same way he'd borrowed money from her, without any real thought. They'd done this for years. Those years were behind them, however.

"I'll manage," she said. "I don't mind walking, either." She couldn't sit here all evening. "Was there something you wanted?"

He turned on the boy charm that she'd once adored but was now more a source of irritation. "You never called me for coffee. I thought I might take you to dinner."

"You don't have any money, remember?" she said. Now, thanks to him, neither did she.

He ramped up the charm. "I can swing takeout for two from a drive through."

She could think of lots of reasons why having dinner with him would be a bad idea. Dallas had told her flat out that he'd mind if she went for coffee with Tim again. He'd mind the idea of her having dinner with him even more.

She was about to refuse. Then, she recalled Marsh's words. *"I never once asked her to turn off her feelings for him. We had a different relationship between us, that's all."*

She liked the relationship she was developing with Dallas a lot more than the one she'd had with Tim. It was more mature. More equal. And so, so much more fun. Loving a man was far different from loving a boy. Dallas really didn't have anything to worry about.

But she and Tim had grown up together. They were always going to have friends in common. Their mothers knew each other quite well, and for years had expected to share grandchildren between them. That didn't mean he got to drop in and out of her life for the rest of her days, screwing things up for her whenever his life was a mess. She had no business letting him do it, either. Marsh was right—Tim was a taker, not a giver. When she looked at him, she felt nothing but negative emotions. She didn't want to feel this way about him forever. They needed to set a few things straight between them as to what their relationship moving forward would be. He'd never been a very good listener, so she'd have to find a way to make sure he understood there'd be no turning back.

Letting him into her personal space—space she shared with Dallas—felt wrong, however. They'd eat in public and she'd tell Dallas all about it the minute he called.

"Grand is a small town, and if we're both going to live here, it doesn't need to be awkward. We don't have to pretend we don't know each other, but we aren't going to pretend we're friends, either. We need to set boundaries. If we each pay for our own meal, we can go to Lou's Pub. The food is good," she said.

The clouds let go before they reached Yellowstone Drive. Tim parked on the street and they dashed for the door of the pub through sheets of rain that bounced off the pavement. The interior of Lou's was warm, dry, dimly lit, and smelled of stale beer and fried food, exactly the same as most pubs.

Lou's was almost empty. Simone and three of her girlfriends were drinking and playing a loud game of darts. Luke and Zack McGregor, two of the brothers who owned the Wagging Tongue Ranch, shot pool while their wives cheered them on. Tim chose a table near the back, away from the racket.

"Just like old times," he said, smiling across the table at her.

"This isn't like old times at all," she replied. He could forget that idea. She doubted if she'd ever get past the anger.

A pretty brunette with bright purple stripes threaded through her high ponytail brought them their menus.

"Hi, Hannah," she said, dimples flashing. She eyed Tim with curiosity and a certain degree of reserve, reminding Hannah she really was going to have to talk to Dallas the minute she saw him so she could explain. Small-town gossip grew legs fast. "The barbequed bacon and onion burger with sweet potato fries is on special tonight."

"Sounds excellent."

"We'll take two," Tim chimed in.

"Separate checks," Hannah added.

They chatted about the people they'd known in Bozeman and friends from Sweetheart they'd gone to school with while they waited for their food. Hannah excused herself to make a trip to the ladies' room.

Simone entered as she was washing her hands. The other woman had been drinking and the high heels she teetered on posed a serious risk to her health. She closed the ladies' room door and leaned against it, one murderous shoe skidding a few inches on the white ceramic tile floor. Hannah couldn't be sure who was holding up what. Her shirt slipped off one shoulder to reveal a butterfly tattoo.

"What are you doing, Hannah?" Simone sighed, sound-

197

ing a whole lot more sober than she appeared. "It'll be all over Grand that you're here with an old boyfriend while Dallas is out of town. You ruined it for Dallie and me. Are you trying to ruin your chances with him, too?"

Hannah would have been offended except Simone's concern appeared genuine, even if mercenary. Not to mention, there'd been nothing between him and Simone, at least according to Dallas, and Hannah had no reason not believe him.

"What makes you think Tim's an old boyfriend?" she asked.

"He hasn't exactly been silent about how he knows you," Simone said. "The whole town is talking about it. He applied for a job at Powell Construction and your name came up. Word has it he used you as a reference to get an apartment from Angus McKillop. Tracey McKenzie was in the shop having her hair done on Wednesday. She told me her brother-in-law was at the taproom the other night. He said your boyfriend and Dallas had words before you threw him out. Tonight is going to make people wonder."

The speed with which news traveled in small towns never failed to amaze. "If Tracey's brother-in-law meant he saw Tim and Dallas speaking to each other, then yes. I'm not sure I'd call it having words, though. And as for me throwing Tim out..." Well, that part kind of happened, so she left it at that.

Simone aimed a finger at her. "Dallas might be laid back

and casual, but he's not the one you have to watch out for. His friend Ryan was at the Wayside when you were there the other morning and he's been asking questions. If he doesn't like you, you're done."

Hannah had a hazy recollection of seeing Ryan that morning. She might have said hello to him too, although she wasn't sure. Had he said something to Dallas about her being there with Tim? If so, then why hadn't Dallas said something about it to her? Was that why he'd had such a bad day at work—not because of the farming accident, or at least not entirely? Was it why he'd given her so much space the rest of the week?

And then, she got annoyed. She'd done nothing wrong. She wasn't sneaking around. She'd chosen to speak with Tim in public precisely because she had nothing to hide. She would have felt guilty about it if she'd met with him in private.

"Girls like us don't get this kind of chance every day," Simone continued. Her face, slapped by stark, overhead lighting, looked as tired as the worn washroom fixtures. She moved away from the door and toward one of the stalls. "Dallas has money. It helps that he's handsome, too. There are lots of women around here who'd happily take your place. Don't throw it away."

Hannah had gotten past her first flush of guilt and moved on to indignation. Yes, she should have told him she'd had coffee with Tim. If he'd had a problem with it, however, then he should have come right out and asked her about it. Meanwhile, he was a good-looking doctor who'd once been a stripper. He had billions of dollars and he was happy to spend it on others because he liked people and he liked to help them. Simone was right in that other women weren't going to care whether or not he was in a relationship, either.

But Hannah honestly didn't know if he was. If they were. They hadn't talked about it. She'd simply made an assumption. Another Marsh-ism surfaced. *"Bringing you here means you're someone special to him."*

It squelched any doubts. If she'd learned one thing about Dallas in the short while she'd known him, it was that he always put others first. He'd never lead anyone on. If he was with her at all it was because she was important to him. She was as sure of him as she was that the sun would rise in the east. He deserved to have the same level of confidence in her.

Because she loved him. It might not have been love at first sight on her part, but he'd definitely worked his way into her heart when she wasn't looking. Then, he'd done what he did best. He'd gathered up all the broken bits and pieces and stitched them back together, leaving her with a new and improved model that had plenty of room.

"I don't care about Dallas's money," she said to Simone, who should be ashamed of herself for thinking that way. How could anyone possibly care more about his money than they did about him?

"Keep telling yourself that," Simone said.

The stall door swung closed. The bolt shot across.

Hannah returned to her table. Their food had arrived while she was gone. She drew her chair up to the heavy slab table and set her elbows on either side of her plate. She tucked her laced fingers under her chin and weighed Simone's unsolicited concerns against Marsh's wise words.

She didn't have to allow anyone else to set the terms for what her relationship with Tim would be. What Grand thought didn't matter. And Dallas, whose opinion did, would have to trust her. The same way she trusted him.

Tim dipped a sweet potato fry in curried mayonnaise and popped it into his mouth. "The food here is fantastic. You should think about adding a menu to the taproom. You'd give this place a real run for its money."

Competing with a place like Lou's Pub had never been part of her business model. He knew that. She'd explained it to him. They'd argued more than once over it, too.

Maybe she didn't listen to him all that well, either.

"Let's talk about those boundaries," she said.

Chapter Fifteen

Dallas

DALLAS GOT HANNAH'S text a few minutes after the helicopter set down at Custer County airport the following Sunday. It was hard to say how urgent it was—she'd known he couldn't be reached, so what did it mean that she'd left it?

He'd hoped to be home early enough to visit the nursing home with her, but they'd been delayed at one of the ranch's many outposts. The men were overworked and short-handed, rounding up range cattle to get them ready for market. He hadn't done any serious ranch work since he was a teenager, and other than he now had the sorest ass in Montana from riding an ATV over rugged terrain for two days, it had been fun.

He frowned at the text. She wasn't one of those women who couldn't let a guy down face-to-face, was she? He remembered the unreturned phone calls after their first brush with romance, and the way she'd dodged him for months before he finally wised up, and his frown deepened. His gut said the potential was there.

He skipped past her message and proceeded to the twenty-three voice mails also requiring his attention. He listened to them from the back of Dan's county-owned work SUV as they drove the ten miles from the small county airport to the ranch. He got to the sixth message, the one from the nursing home, then sat up abruptly.

"What's wrong?" Ryan asked from the front passenger seat, noticing the change.

"My friend Marsh passed away." Hannah had to be devastated, too. The message said he'd passed away last Sunday—which might account for her text. The timing was right.

According to his phone, it was a few minutes past five o'clock. If she'd gone to the nursing home, even though Marsh was no longer there, she'd be home by now. He tried to call her, but the cell signal kept cutting out, which was just as well. He didn't need his friends listening in on their conversation, particularly if he was wrong, and Marsh's passing wasn't behind the text message she'd sent him.

They passed under the sign for the Endeavour Ranch. Once inside the main house, he dragged his backpack and bedroll through the gigantic common room and stumbled into his private quarters. He dumped the whole lot in the laundry room off the kitchen, planning to deal with them later, and caught a whiff of himself. A week of scrubbing down in the Tongue hadn't done much beyond the basics as far as personal hygiene was concerned.

He showered and shaved, then he called Hannah. Now that his initial paranoia had passed, he was hungry to see her.

"Hey, I just got your text," he said when she answered. He put her on speakerphone while he got dressed. "It sounded urgent. What's up?"

A long pause clenched his heart in a vice. "Marsh passed away last Sunday. I asked what arrangements had been made for him, and they told me he'd left instructions for cremation and no funeral."

"I heard. The home left me a message. Look. I haven't eaten yet and I'm starving. Are you hungry? Why don't I grab us some takeout and bring it over?" He rummaged through a drawer in search of clean socks, working hard not to sound too relieved, because the knot in his stomach hadn't gone away yet. Things were far from settled between them.

"I am."

He couldn't tell a thing from her tone. "I'll see you in an hour."

He placed an order for burgers at Lou's Pub, and a half hour later, stopped in to pick it up. The pub was busier than usual for a Sunday night and Leila told him it would be another fifteen minutes.

He scanned the crowd while he waited, not really paying attention until he saw Tim Ryder, sitting alone, nursing a beer. He was already moving before his brain could advise he use caution.

"Mind if I join you?" he asked, then sat down before Ryder could answer.

This was someone Hannah had loved. Maybe still did. And he'd like to know why. All Dallas had heard about him were the negative things, but very few people were truly all bad and Hannah's judgment was better than that. Misguided loyalty was her Achilles' heel.

The other man picked at his fries. "Suit yourself."

"How'd the job interview go?" Dallas asked, to let it be known that he and Hannah talked to each other. Their brief phone call hadn't filled in any blanks and he was feeling a touch insecure.

"It's mine if I want it. Thanks for asking."

He detected sarcasm but no outright hostility. "I thought it might be a good idea to clear the air between you and me without Hannah around to interfere."

"How do you suggest we do that? Pistols at dawn? Fisticuffs at the local gentlemen's club?" Ryder asked, a glimmer of humor apparent in the wry twist of his mouth. "Is that how you rich people do it these days?"

Again, with the money—as if that was all he had going for him. "I'm a doctor," Dallas said mildly. "We prefer talking before resorting to violence."

"That's a relief. You want to talk. Go ahead."

Dallas went with what he was most curious about. "Tell me why you think you'd be better for Hannah."

"You mean, justify why you're better for her than me."

Tim dropped his fry and wiped his fingers on his napkin. "Okay. You have money and I don't. I get it. You can take care of her and I've done a crap job of that. But all I need is a break. Besides, I know her a lot better than you do. She doesn't care about money, you know. She and I argued over the original business plan for the brewery from the beginning because she wants it to be a community hangout and that's not a moneymaker. We hit a rough patch right about then. She was working all the time, saving money for a project I didn't believe in, and I was lonely and bored and ignored. Neither one of us is perfect. If you hadn't happened along, we would have gotten through it."

That wasn't quite the way Hannah told the story, but Ryder was entitled to his own take on things, although he'd glossed over one other detail that was worth pointing out.

"If she's not interested in me for my money, then how am I possibly interfering in you two working things out?" Dallas asked.

"She made it clear when we had dinner together last week that she intends to give you a chance. I'm not allowed to contact her or visit the taproom for the next six months. After that though, the gloves come off."

Dallas didn't miss the smug dig about dinner. Maybe he should have been more specific when he told her he'd mind if she went out for coffee. The six-month moratorium was far more interesting, though.

"So... it's a competition," he said thoughtfully.

Ryder lifted his glass. "May the better man win."

Dallas's last bits of jealousy and fear vanished. His churning gut settled. Maybe he wasn't all that great at reading women sometimes, but he understood Hannah. She hadn't been able to convince the guy to push off, so she'd bought time for him to figure it out for himself. There was no question she had some issues to work through where he was concerned—she'd lent him a thousand dollars, which made no sense at all—but she'd been finished with him before she ever met Dallas, and deep down, she'd known it. Dallas would stake his entire fortune on that.

Lou pushed through the swinging doors that led to the kitchen. A white chef's apron covered his rounded midriff. He waved to Dallas from the cash register at the front counter, signaling his order was ready.

Dallas tapped fisted knuckles on the table as he rose. "Nice talking to you."

"Likewise," Ryder said.

Dallas had just finished paying for his food order when Simone showed up at his elbow. Her T-shirt was too tight, her skirt was too short, and her makeup, too thick. He was so not in the mood for her right now, but he hid his impatience. She was another example of someone who wasn't all bad. Her life hadn't gone according to plan. Some people picked themselves up easier than others and she did her best.

"I figured you'd be over at Hannah's by now," she said. "Didn't you get back from vacation this afternoon?"

Lou handed the two white paper takeout bags over the counter to him. He held them up to show them to Simone. "I'm on my way."

Simone eyeballed the ceiling for the briefest of seconds. "Honestly, Dallie. You have plenty of money. Couldn't you treat a girl to something better than pub food? No offense, Lou."

"None taken." Lou shrugged and moved off.

"Next time," Dallas said to her, although he had no such intentions. The things Hannah cared about—and deserved—couldn't be bought.

"Wait." Simone caught his arm. She wavered, clearly struggling with an internal dilemma. "Hannah's a good person." She jerked her chin in Ryder's direction. "Whatever he told you about her, don't believe it."

Dallas didn't know about that. He'd heard a few things he believed. The clearest takeaway he'd gotten from their brief conversation was that Hannah chose to be kinder to Ryder in the way she ended things with him than he'd been to her.

That natural kindness was why Dallas had fallen for her so hard and so fast. He couldn't expect her to not care what became of an old boyfriend. If anything, he loved her the more for it. He planned to tell her so, too.

"Thank you. You're a good person, too," he told Simone, and he meant it. She had nothing to gain, and yet, she'd made the effort to help Hannah out.

It would be a while before he trusted her with a haircut again, though.

Just in case.

✳

Hannah

HANNAH RAN DOWN the stairs and threw open the back door to let Dallas in when he called to say he'd arrived.

Tousled black curls and warm hazel eyes were the first things she noticed. Sun- and wind-reddened cheeks and chapped hands made it apparent he'd spent the last week outdoors. A denim jacket and button-down flannel shirt made an already wide chest seem that much broader. Wrangler jeans topped a pair of worn leather boots. He looked more like a ranch hand and less like a doctor. Both looks suited him equally well, although she liked him best when he was stripped naked. He carried two bags of takeout.

He peered over his shoulder into the brightly lit parking lot behind him rather than offering her the kiss she'd looked forward to with huge expectations. "Why is there a REST IN PEACE sign in your truck's windshield?" he asked.

Because she'd thought it might make him laugh when he saw it.

"The FREE TO A GOOD HOME sign didn't work and the town asked me to move the remains off the street. They'd had complaints," she said, working past her disappointment over not getting a kiss. She was the one who'd asked for space, after all.

"When's your birthday?" he asked. "I'll buy you another second-hand, rusted-out piece of junk and maybe you can Frankenstein it back to life."

"Not until May, so save your money, big spender. I'll buy my own second-hand junker long before then. Besides, I'd rather you give me chocolates and flowers. I'm old-fashioned that way."

She led him up the stairs to the warmth of her apartment. She was so happy to have Dallas home that she couldn't take her eyes off him. All of the positive emotions she associated with love jockeyed into position inside her heart. Happiness. Warmth. A sense of belonging.

Puzzled hazel eyes smiled back at her over the way she was staring at him. "Do I have something stuck between my teeth?"

She reached up without thinking and held his cheeks with her hands. She brushed his mouth with her thumbs. She might as well get it all out. She'd been holding it in for a week and there was no time like the present.

"I love you," she blurted out, then in the same breath she added, "I had dinner with Tim last Sunday night," because she'd been hanging on to that, too.

The two takeout bags hit the counter. "I don't care."

A split second later, she was in Dallas's arms. She got the

kiss she'd been waiting so impatiently for. When their lips parted, she couldn't remember what they'd been talking about.

She tugged a lock of his hair, getting her thoughts back in order. "You don't care that I love you?"

"I definitely care about that." He kissed the tip of her nose. "I'd planned to say it to you first, though. Thanks for stealing my thunder."

"I'll make it up to you," she said, relieved he didn't seem at all interested in the rest of her announcement. "You can say it to me all night. I promise not to say it to you again."

"It's okay. You can tell me you love me as much as you like. Besides, I loved you first. I fell in love with you the minute I walked through the door at the Campbellses and saw this beautiful girl talking to Blaise. I spent the days leading up to the wedding trying to figure out how to get you to pay more attention to me." He held her tighter. "But do I dare ask what brought this on?"

"Something Marsh said." Sadness muted her joy. "He told me I'd been gifted with plenty of feelings to go around. It took me a while, but I finally figured out I also get to choose how I want them distributed, and it seems they're heavily skewed in your favor. I don't know when I fell in love with you," she confessed. "I wish I did. The potential was definitely there at the wedding, though. I think that's why you scared me so much. I was a mess and you seemed so sure of yourself."

"I was sure of what I wanted, not of myself," he corrected her. "Big difference there. I also know you had dinner with Tim, by the way. Maybe I do care about that, after all." He threaded his fingers under the braid at the nape of her neck, tilting her face upward. "You can make that up to me, too."

"You had no reason to worry. He and I were long overdue for a real conversation. One that didn't involve me imagining how good it would feel to break his nose, I mean. The opportunity came up and I took advantage of it."

"Talking is generally the better option," Dallas agreed. "Although, granted, breaking his nose has crossed my mind more than once, too. But having dinner with him isn't the part you have to make up to me. You told him he only has to stay away from you for six months. That doesn't give me nearly enough time to step up my game. First, I have to convince you to move in with me. Then, I have to ease you into the subject of marriage. I'd like to avoid stirring up local interest in that. They're already way too invested in the Endeavour as it is, and if our first baby arrives before nine months are up, people will talk. If we want eight or ten kids though, we need to get started."

She loved the silliness of him. And yet he always managed to focus on what really mattered without the disagreement escalating to shouting and tears. A man who could patch up a bullet wound on his best friend knew how to stay calm. "You talked to Tim. That's how you knew I had dinner with him."

"He was at Lou's when I stopped in for takeout. I decided to check out the opposition. FYI, I really did want to break his nose."

She nestled deeper into Dallas's arms. "He's not your competition."

"Hell, no. That was obvious two minutes into the conversation. I doubt if it will take him six months to figure it out, either. I give him two at the most. Even that's being generous." He kissed the top of her head. "I love you, Hannah. I've missed you so much these past two weeks. I couldn't get you out of my head."

"I asked for one night to sort myself out. The two weeks are on you."

She pressed her cheek against the side of his throat and breathed in Tom Ford. A memory stirred. He'd asked her to dance at Alayna and Patterson's party. Her first impression of him was that he was so sexy and smart. She'd thought he'd help her prove she knew how to be bold and have fun. She'd been right on both counts. But he'd also shown her how to take advantage of opportunities, and to go after what she wanted, without losing sight of what was important.

His hand began a slow slide under the hem of her shirt. "You're wrong, you know," she said, before things could progress any further.

The hand paused in the sensitive area between her hip and her breast. "For argument's sake, about what?"

"Eight or ten kids. We should aim for a dozen."

"That sounds like it's going to require a lot of cuddling on my part. Not that I'm complaining. But we should probably negotiate this. You're going to have to up your game, too," he said. "How do you plan to do that?"

She smiled into those intense, hazel eyes and let all the love she felt for him slide into hers. "You've forgotten how good I am at games. Let me remind you," she said. Taking his hand, she led him toward the bedroom.

"Follow me, Dr. Tucker. Practice makes perfect."

Epilogue

Dallas

DALLAS BUMPED THE stroller backward over the little lip in the base of the doorframe and tugged it behind him as he entered the taproom. He and the kids were headed for the playground up the street to wait for their mother to finish up for the day just as soon as they got to give her their present. Hannah had left the ranch before breakfast and it was now almost suppertime. They were taking her out to celebrate her birthday.

The taproom was empty. She had to be in the brewery out back. Judging by the smell, she was perfecting a fresh batch of her maple brew. The sweet smell of the syrup was offset by the damp odor of barley and sharp suggestion of hops. He had no idea how that combination could turn into something so amazing, but the women who came for Wednesday ladies' nights had a decided preference for it.

The change in management at the Grand Master Brewery two years ago hadn't hurt business at all. It was booming, in fact. Hannah had expanded its service to include food, but the taproom didn't carry a full menu and most likely, never would. The intention was to keep it community-centric and give people lots of opportunity to mingle. She also hosted numerous fundraising events for the hospital and nursing home. Installing Ford Shannahan as manager had been another stroke of genius on her part. Not only was he a real people person, he helped with the heavy lifting.

"Hello?" Dallas called out.

"Mommy?" Benny sang, taking his cue from his dad.

The three-year-old occupied the front seat of the stroller, gripping the guardrail and kicking his sneakered heels against the footrest. He looked just like his proud dad, right down to the dark curls and hazel eyes, but he had his mommy's sweet personality and engaging smile. He was cautious and caring, too. He watched over one-year-old Rose, quiet for the moment in the rear section of the stroller under the blue and yellow canopy, and couldn't stand it if she cried.

Rose, on the other hand, while a junior version of her mom, was more of an opportunist, like her dad. No caution there. Hannah had already warned him that their daughter wouldn't be stripping her way through medical school, and he was to stop playing stripper music for her. He pointed out that Rose would have plenty of money to fund her education, so if she ended up as a stripper, it would be because she liked to dance. Then he'd proceeded to play the music for Hannah, one thing led to another, and well, here they were. Baby number three was on the way any day now.

Hannah's mother was flying in from Sweetheart that evening to help with Benny and Rose until after the new one arrived. Ryan planned to pick her up at the airport in Billings and fly her by helicopter to the ranch. Hannah's relationship with her mother explained so many things. Tessa Brand was excellent with small children, and loved the grandkids to pieces, but when it came to looking after herself, she was at a bit of a disadvantage. After the death of Hannah's father in a boating accident on Flathead Lake, Tessa had looked to her children for support rather than the other way around.

The door between the taproom and the brewery swung open. Hannah maneuvered her very pregnant belly through it. She rubbed the small of her back, glanced up, caught his eye, and smiled. Dallas lost his train of thought, as he often did at moments like this, when he was struck by how beautiful she was and couldn't believe his good luck. The kids were forgotten. He was transported back to the first moment he set eyes on her, at a friend's pre-wedding party, when he'd taken one look and known in his heart that she was the woman for him.

The money continued to be a big PITA. However, it did come with perks. He loved life on the ranch. It was a great place to raise a big family—and they'd made an excellent start on that. He liked being a country doctor. It was all he'd ever wanted to do.

Well. He had one other thing he was good at.

"Hey, honey. We have a birthday present for you," he said.

"This should be good. Although I can't see how you could top last year," she replied. They'd made her a chocolate and coffee-flavored cake and decorated it to look like a frothy mug of stout beer.

"Hold that thought."

He lifted Benny out of the stroller and set him on his feet before rescuing little Rose.

"What in the world…" Hannah exclaimed when she saw what they were wearing. Benny sported a tiny tearaway police uniform. Rose wore a wee pink bikini top decorated with miniature pink tassels. Dallas had stenciled a G-string on her diaper with a pink Magic Marker.

He grabbed his phone. Joe Cocker began to croon "You Can Leave Your Hat On." Benny immediately got into the spirit of things. He jiggled around the room, shaking his groove thing. Dallas wasn't sure what it was Rose was trying to accomplish. Her bottom bobbed up and down but her rhythm sucked. She definitely wasn't the one Hannah had to worry about making a career out of stripping.

Hannah was laughing so hard by now, tears dripped off her eyelashes and onto her cheeks. Dallas handed her two five-dollar bills just before Benny's big finale. The uniform came off to reveal Batman training pants. Both kids toddled over so their mother could tuck the bills in their undies, as they'd been coached, although Rose was most likely following her big brother.

"Worst father ever," Hannah said, wiping her eyes with the back of her hand.

He scooped her into a bear hug despite her massive belly making it awkward. "But best husband, am I right?"

She wrapped her arms around his neck. Soft blue eyes, hazy with love, gazed into his. "The best," she assured him. "And when you give me the adult strip show version later tonight, I'll be the luckiest woman alive."

The End

Don't miss the next book in the Grand, Montana series, *The Montana Rancher*!

Join Tule Publishing's newsletter for more great reads and weekly deals!

If you enjoyed *The Montana Doctor*,
you'll love the next books in…

The Grand, Montana series

Book 1: *The Montana Sheriff*

Book 2: *The Montana Doctor*

Book 3: *The Montana Rancher*
Coming in June 2022

Book 4: *The Cowboy's Christmas Baby*
Coming in October 2022

Available now at your favorite online retailer!

More books by Paula Altenburg

The Montana McGregor Brothers series

Book 1: *The Rancher Takes a Family*

Book 2: *The Rancher's Secret Love*

Book 3: *The Rancher's Proposal*

A Sweetheart Brand series

Book 1: *Her Montana Brand*

Book 2: *The Cowboy's Brand*

Book 3: *Branded by the Cowboy*

Available now at your favorite online retailer!

About the Author

USA Today Bestselling Author Paula Altenburg lives in rural Nova Scotia, Canada with her husband and two sons. A former aviation and aerospace professional, Paula now writes contemporary romance and fantasy with romantic elements.

Thank you for reading

The Montana Doctor

If you enjoyed this book, you can find more from all our great authors at TulePublishing.com, or from your favorite online retailer.

TULE
PUBLISHING

Printed in Great Britain
by Amazon